M000307671

ACKNOWLEDGMENTS

With most heartfelt thanks to Amy Spitz, for freelance developmental editing. I am deeply grateful to my dear friend and writer Nick Marsh, who provided superb advice and editing suggestions.

And lastly, to my readers—all of my love to you.

Cynthia

ALSO BY CYNTHIA WILLIAMS

Growing Up in the D: My Grandfather, My Mother, and Me

This book is a work of fiction. Names, characters, places and incidents either are products of the author's imagination or are used fictitiously. Any resemblance to actual events or locales or persons living or dead, is entirely coincidental.

Copyright © 2016 Cynthia Williams
All rights reserved.

No part of this publication may be reproduced, stored in a retrieval system, or transmitted in any form or by any means, electronic, mechanical, photocopying, recording, or otherwise, without written permission of the publisher.

ISBN: 978-0-578-13174-0

The Whispering Pines Inn

by
Cynthia Williams

Illustration by

Richard Cruger

In memory of William T. Spencer, one of the great blessings in my life.

I whispered, 'I am too young',
And then, 'I am old enough';
Wherefore I threw a penny
To find out if I might love.
'Go and love, go and love, young man,
If the lady be young and fair.'
Ah, penny, brown penny, brown penny,
I am looped in the loops of her hair.

O love is the crooked thing,
There is nobody wise enough
To find out all that is in it,
For he would be thinking of love
Till the stars had run away
And the shadows eaten the moon.
Ah, penny, brown penny, brown penny,
One cannot begin it too soon.

-W.B. YEATS

I lay on the bowsprit, facing astern, with
   the water foaming into spume under me,
   the masts with every sail white in the
   moonlight, towering high above me.
I became drunk with the beauty and singing
   rhythm of it, and for a moment I lost
   myself----actually lost my life.
I was set free!
I dissolved in the sea, became white sails and
   flying spray, became beauty and rhythm,
   became moonlight and the ship and the
   high dim-starred sky!
I belonged, without past or future, within
   peace and unity and a wild joy, within
   something greater than my own life, or the
   life of Man, to Life itself!
To God, if you want to put it that way.
            -Eugene O'Neill, *Long Day's Journey into Night*

The Whispering Pines Inn

CHAPTER 1

THE READING OF THE WILL
March 1963

The news came to Margaret Sanders from a niece in Brooklyn. Marvin Feldman, grandson of Irving Feldman and an heir to the Feldman entertainment empire had died of an apparent heart attack in a Manhattan hotel at the age of thirty-nine. The niece sent a couple of press clippings a few days later, short squibs, nothing Margaret didn't already know. Marvin's premature demise was not unexpected. Margaret or as most of her friends called her, Maggie, had heard rumors, rumblings. In actuality, Marvin Feldman died from drugs, alcohol and poor choices—a life dissipated by a desperate and futile search for pleasure and happiness.

Feldman Holdings began as a dinner theatre in a northern Michigan circus tent. Nathan Zingerman was Feldman's confidant and trusted friend. The corporation, under Nathan's entertainment expertise and investment savvy, expanded into local movie houses, diners, roller skating rinks and, eventually, resorts. Even wax museums and legitimate theatre productions.

The empire grew from northern Michigan to the Smoky Mountains and Poconos. In its heyday, the Whispering Pines was a crown jewel in the Feldman entertainment dynasty. But, with the Great Depression and WWII, the Feldman properties fell on hard times. After Irving's death, the Feldman descendants picked the carcass clean as vultures.

Marvin, the baby of the family who had never left his northern Michigan roots, scored somewhat of a coup, when by default, he inherited the Whispering Pines (i.e. valuable lake frontage) and a trust fund in which the principal was not accessible until Marvin's thirtieth birthday. Located on Lake Charlevoix and surrounded by huge white pine trees, the former resort used to sit on 100 acres but now the lakefront lots had been sold off and 500 feet of frontage remained. It had a dock and a diving raft. The raft was made of oil barrels with a wooden pine platform. The one barrel was rusty and had a leak so the entire raft listed to one side making the raft an allegory for the Inn itself. Most summer evenings you could still hear the plaintive cries of the loons on the lake. One had the sense that it was inexorably retreating, going back to nature-the sun and the elements were reclaiming it.

The Whispering Pines Inn was formerly the Whispering Pines Resort back in the 1920s. It welcomed visitors from Chicago, California and New York City with the words, "Know Thyself" inscribed over the main entrance. Known by the locals as the Pines, presently it was affectionately referred to as "The Falling Pines."

The Inn was situated between Charlevoix and East Jordan on a bluff overlooking the south arm of Lake Charlevoix in Charlevoix County. The Inn had two floors, 14 rooms, one large apartment, four cabins, five cottages and an office.

The legal correspondence arrived by certified mail on heavy bond stationery. The presence of Margaret Sanders was required at the reading of the Last Will and Testament of Marvin Feldman. Local estate and probate attorney, Bradford Mitchell was handling the estate. "I need this like I need a hole in my head," Maggie thought. She tried to buttonhole old lawyer Mitchell on the street in East Jordan, to take care of business on an informal basis. He would have none of it. "He's going to milk this cash cow until it's dry," she said to herself.

The day of the reading of the Last Will and Testament finally arrived. Maggie showed up at Mr. Mitchell, Esq.'s office at 9:50 A.M. and was escorted into a spacious conference room. "My God. He's even cleaned this out," Maggie observed. Present, gathered and accounted for in the conference room was the most eclectic, sundry and assorted collection of twelve people ever to be found in East Jordan history. Maggie just stood and stared, mouth agape. Before she could properly assess the situation and reorient herself in time and place, Attorney Mitchell bustled into the room and announced, "It's 10 A.M. We might as well begin."

At a silent signal, a secretary brought a pitcher of ice water and distributed glasses of ice water, small yellow writing pads and ballpoint pens. "I am attorney Bradford Mitchell, Executor of the estate of Marvin Feldman." Several present leaned forward, sipped water, straightened dresses or adjusted ties in anticipation of the tremendous windfall which they were about to receive.

After an interminable recitation of standard legal boilerplate, Mitchell got to the heart of the matter. "To my friends Jimbo, Skip and Chandler, I leave my timeshare in Montauk, Long Island."

"To my jockey Rudolpho, I leave my polo pony, Thumper."

"To my special friend Amy, (who squealed with delight) I leave my gold chains, with instructions to pawn them at Ralph's on 48th St., next to the bodega."

"To my driver Boris, I leave my sand buggy."

"To Chandler, who is my size eleven, I leave my collection of Gucci shoes and slippers."

"To my art investment adviser Frederick, I leave my Rothko forgery."

It went on and on. "What the hell!" Maggie thought. "What about the Michigan blue chips—the utilities, the railroads, the banks? I could never imagine that one person, in so short a lifetime, would collect such a worthless, useless bunch of crap."

And mercilessly, the reading of the Last Will and Testament of Marvin Feldman droned on. At one point, out of false empathy, special friend Amy leaned over, patted Maggie on the arm and said, "Don't worry. I'm sure you'll get something."

Maggie had descended into a sort of stupor when she heard her name. Attorney Mitchell cleared his throat and began reading the bequest again. Years earlier, Maggie worked as a bookkeeper for three years in Petoskey at the Sperry Hotel after being laid off from managing the Whispering Pines Inn. "Isn't this a kick in the pants?" Then the news came about the inheritance.

"To our devoted family friend and faithful employee Margaret Sanders, I leave the Whispering Pines Inn, and all property attached thereto, including but not limited to, any and all assets, real and personal property, furniture, furnishings, equipment, appurtenances name, goodwill and any other property, of whatever nature, to do with as she sees fit."

After reading a few final standard clauses, Bradford Mitchell announced, "Thank you, ladies and gentlemen. That concludes the reading of the Last Will and Testament of Marvin Feldman. I will be in touch with each of you to keep you apprised of the status of the probate of the estate." Maggie stood and waited patiently to exit the conference room, amid grumblings and several dirty looks. As she reached the outer office door, Attorney Mitchell caught up with her and said, "Margaret we need to talk, as soon as possible."

Maggie drove her 1960, red convertible Chevy Impala a little recklessly on the smooth pavement leading to Mr. Mitchell's office in East Jordan. She veered into a parking space outside, hurried inside, and took a seat in the lobby. Maggie had lots of thoughts churning in her head.

She walked into the inner sanctum of his office. "I assume that you will be making arrangements to demolish the Inn and subdivide the property?" Mitchell said.

Mitchell needed some convincing, and Maggie delivered, "Demolish the Inn? No, the Whispering Pines Inn has been the centerpiece of East Jordan for half a century! Generations of East Jordan high school students took their first jobs at the Inn and it is an integral part of the East Jordan economy! It may be decrepit but it's a grand old dame."

"But Maggie, the Inn hasn't been doing so well in a very long time," Mitchell interjected.

"I know the Inn went into a slump in the mid-1950s, but since the Inn is recognized as one of the oldest summer resorts in Charlevoix County, and has a great central location, renovation needs to be considered the next logical step," Maggie said.

"The Inn," Maggie continued, "offers many surprising and inconspicuous things to young people working here and instills in them a strong work ethic. In addition to gaining valuable work experience at the Inn, I am talking about: beachcombing for shells, beach glass, and Petoskey stones, learning to fly fish, star gazing, watching for fireflies at night, spotting a falling star, studying the area's unique geological features, canoeing or kayaking on the lake, hunting for morel mushrooms, walking in the woods at daybreak, cooking on a wood fire, and sailing."

"I see what you're saying," Mitchell replied.

Maggie moved in the late winter of 1963 and hired her staff. They went room to room and found evidence of kids breaking in and some hard partying in the large dining room.

MAGGIE AND THE EARLY DAYS OF THE WHISPERING PINES INN

Margaret Sanders was born July 17, 1920 and was an East Jordan native. She was an only child and her father worked as a journeyman ironworker at East Jordan Iron Works. East Jordan Iron Works made manhole covers worldwide. Margaret's mother, Grace, passed away when she was six-years old and she was raised by her father and loving grandparents. Margaret started working at the Inn during its heyday as a housekeeper, and was mesmerized, enthralled by the hustle, bustle and big city guests who came from Boston, Chicago, Kansas City, Des Moines, Minneapolis, and New York.

After working for a year in Detroit at J. L. Hudson's Department Store, Maggie returned to northern Michigan in the late-fall of 1942. In early 1943, everything was going fine until the day she overheard her bookkeeper Dorothy say, "I just can't seem to get the hang of this dang bookkeeping work, and by the way I quit." Beleaguered and overwhelmed with bills, Maggie took over the bookkeeping and the housekeeping duties.

The big old rambling Inn and what used to be a summer resort from the 1920s, had green board and shake shingles. Large white snowball bushes and faded pink hydrangeas surrounded the front porch. Faded, crooked, chipped green shutters showed the passage of time and there was a prominent stone fireplace off the dining room. The Potawatomi Indian rugs, baskets and artifacts could be seen throughout the resort. The lobby was a beehive of energy and activity in its heyday. Guests enjoyed badminton or a rousing game of croquet on the front lawn.

All the memories came back to Maggie, some that she tried to avoid. Her style was to just keep moving, but it never worked when she thought about her mother, her father and Burt who she missed and who had left a void in her life. Feeling the stillness of a warm, summer night, remembering the summer days as they became shorter, and Burt's enchanted embrace, Maggie longed for her youth and the times she could share her heart with Burt.

Burt would always say, "Maggie, don't ever let the world try to rob us of the tender affection we have for each other."

She remembered being curled up on a porch swing in her overall shorts and strappy sandals. She watched fireflies' lighting up the darkness with excitement and carrying on in the most astonishing manner. Maggie found great comfort in listening to the katydids and crickets on many summer nights on the porch of the Inn. This was a place where she could look up to the sky at night, and immediately locate the constellations. She knew that there were 100 million stars in our galaxy and the naked eye could see 2,000...

It was 1963 now and lately it's been just a few old geezers and a lady crossing the lobby so slowly she left a translucent snail trail. The lady's name was Adeline Dawson, a spinster who resided on the adjacent acreage. Adeline had lived there all of her life. That was 85 years.

Back in 1951, her nephew Mortimer moved to California and his son, Wayne went to the University of California-Davis and studied enology, the making of wine.

One summer, in 1955, Wayne visited for a month and talked Adeline into starting a vineyard. Initially, she was very enthusiastic as this would be her legacy.

The only problem was, Wayne barely passed his classes in wine-making and as more and more caterpillar worms seized the grape-vines, his dreams of exploring the world of Bordeaux's and Chateaubriand came to a crashing halt. He returned to slinging fudge out of a food cart for the summer down by the East Jordan boat dock.

Down by the lake, near the Inn, there used to be a huge permanent pier with a band shell. Now the only thing that was left was a few pilings that were good for catching fish like bass. Some of the local taverns were the Boogaloo Lounge and Wet Willie's in Cheboygan. Wet Willie's was formerly named the Country Stampede and prior to that Club Avalanche.

CHAPTER 2

BURT
1931

"If your eyes were the ocean I'd be marooned forever." -Burt

Burt Armstrong was a friend of Maggie's from their childhood days in East Jordan. Burt was born June 11, 1919. Burt always looked after Maggie like an older brother. Burt would play hide and seek but never look for Maggie which made her confused. Finally, she caught on, and was infuriated with him. During the intense, hot days of summer, before World War II captured the attention of the country, Burt would take Maggie out in his green, wood rowboat and instruct her to row the boat. Burt would sit in the back with his legs propped up and his arms straddling the sides like an Egyptian Pharaoh. He would secretly drop the anchor off the back and watch her as she tried to row. She would splash him with the oars and he knew it was time to go in.

THE RUN AWAY ROWBOAT
1932

Accusations flew back and forth. Burt soon came to the realization that he would not bully Maggie into admitting blame for so egregious a nautical mistake as failing to tie off the rowboat. The debate was becoming tedious. Ever vigilant for a new source of amusement, Burt called for a recess to the proceedings and decided to approach the matter from a new tack.

"Would you be satisfied if I could prove beyond a shadow of a doubt whether or not you are telling the truth?" he asked.

"Yeah. I guess," Maggie answered warily.

"OK, come with me. This will just take a minute," Burt said.

"What will just take a minute?" Maggie asked with growing alarm.

"Have you heard of a lie detector? Well, the professional polygraph guys have the sophisticated lie detector machines with all the dials and fancy gizmos just so they can charge big bucks. Actually, the principal behind the lie detector is quite simple. I have been tinkering around in my shed and I believe that I have developed a rudimentary lie detector which gives accurate results." He had her at the term "rudimentary." Who was Maggie to question so intelligent a seventh grader?

As they arrived at the shed, Burt scanned the horizon checking that the coast was clear. Maggie followed him into the shed with a sense of foreboding. It seemed that the shed always played a key role in far-fetched schemes that ended in trouble.

Once inside the shed, Burt rummaged around in a corner and found a cardboard box, "Ah ha!" he exclaimed in satisfaction. From the box he pulled out an old, beat up aluminum bowl. To each side of the bowl was glued a small dish washing sponge. From each sponge ran two feet of frayed wire and these wires merged into a six foot extension cord ending in a two pronged male plug.

Burt handed the bowl device to Maggie. "Here. Just put this on your head," he directed.

"No! It's disgusting," Maggie replied.

"Don't be a sissy. We need to get to the bottom of this matter," Burt declared in as authoritative a voice as he could muster. "You'll be proud to know that you're my first human test subject," he added.

"Hadn't you first better check it out? You know, take it for a test run," Maggie said, trying to humor Burt.

"O. K.," said Burt, now having doubts himself as to the efficacy of his invention. He set the homemade polygraph machine on the cardboard box and, after a few moments of self-doubt, pretended to plug it in. He never intended to plug it in, but Maggie said, "See it is fake," and dared him to plug it in. He really didn't want to, but did anyway. Boom!

Sparks flew from the electrical outlet, an impressive roman candle-like fireworks display. The overhead bulb which had illuminated the shed, flickered and then went out.

A transformer box mounted on an electrical pole out by the road hummed ominously. Burt peered out of a grimy shed window scouting for witnesses and noticed, with dismay that the barn light had gone out as well.

Burt turned to Maggie, "There must be something wrong with the electrical ground. Somebody needs to check that out. C'mon. We should get going," he observed.

Suddenly, he noticed his dad coming out the back door, looking like a madman.

"Come on," he said to Maggie, as he slipped out the side door of the garage, "Let's go see what Jimmy is doing."

"I thought you didn't like Jimmy!?" said Maggie.

"He's not so bad," Burt replied.

Maggie stepped out of the shed and thought, "Burt's absurdities often get the best of him."

There were hundreds of times she wanted to tell him how she felt about him, but for some strange reason she didn't do it. She held back.

She admitted to herself that she liked being with him and all the attention he gave her because she was an only child. Being without siblings intensified her feelings of loneliness.

As a youth, she envied the raucous noise and laughter she heard at many of her friends' homes and wondered what her life would be like if she had a brother or sister to compete with. When Burt charged in, he filled an empty space in her young life.

THE RAFT
SUMMER 1934

Wanting to demonstrate her courage and her stamina, Maggie decided to build a raft in the summer of 1934. She could paddle it out into seven to eight feet of water. It was cut out of a 14 foot cedar log split in two. She was tremendously impressed with boats that had a little cuddy cabin.

One day, as she was paddling the raft into the shore she saw the outhouse on its side in among the bushes and had a brilliant idea. With minimal modifications, she mounted the outhouse in the middle of the raft. She even rigged it so she could paddle the raft while sitting in the outhouse. Later that week, her father forbade her from paddling around Lake Charlevoix. Of course, this did not prevent Maggie taking on a few late night excursions during the summer. She took the raft out at night, likening herself to Amelia Earhart, a symbol of the perseverance and power of American women, and the adventurous spirit so essential to the American persona, whom she learned about in school. The local revelers would see this outhouse float by as they were trying to find their way home. It caused more than one to rethink their amount of alcohol consumption.

CHAPTER 3

SHANTY
1937

When Maggie was a teenager, a lot of people went ice fishing, but she always thought to herself, "If you don't have a shanty[1] it's no fun!"

First, she nailed wooden downhill skis to the side of the family outhouse. Then she dragged it down to Lake Charlevoix and tipped it back up right. She used it as a fishing shanty. The outhouse was her family's primary bathroom way back when she was small. As a teen, her father put in indoor plumbing but he still liked to use the old outhouse because it was quiet and he could sit and think while reading the Petoskey Snooze News Review. Snakes sometimes made an appearance and got you moving!

The law on ice shanties was you must have your name and town where you lived displayed on it. Once her father, Sam, discovered that the outhouse had to have the family name on it, he made Mag-

---

1 "A portable ice fishing shanty is needed especially on the larger lakes. Protection from cold, frigid winds is a must. One that can be easily towed out onto the ice and quickly set up is required. Of course a gas lantern is needed to shed some light inside any shanty and especially so at night."

gie haul it back home.

Maggie told people, "This outhouse is a world traveler and traveled more distance than any outhouse in Charlevoix County."

TO THE HILLS OF EAST JORDAN
1937

Nowhere is there a lovelier country than the Grand Traverse Bay region where our farm was located. Backed by rolling hills and hardwood forests, which the lumberman had not yet stripped, it looked down upon and out across Lake Michigan, clear to the western horizon and southward up the bay itself for many miles to where Traverse City lay hidden in purple haze.

- Rex Bedh, *Personal Exposures* (New York/London: Harper & Brothers, 1940)

The white sand of the beach at East Jordan Park was hot under Burt's feet, and he ran, pulling Maggie into the water with him. They swam out to an old, wooden floating raft. Burt always insisted that Maggie work on perfecting her cannonball. Her memory of that day brought back blue skies, white caps, sailboats, dark rocks in the water, Burt's smiling face and embraces under a large blanket.

"I love you Maggie, I love you darling," Burt whispered.

Maggie gave him a tremulous smile.

"Sure, sure, let's get going," Maggie said.

Burt felt confused. Maggie just wanted to chum around and he didn't understand her and her lack of feelings for him at the time.

Maggie was 17 years old in that summer of 1937. She couldn't fully comprehend what love was all about. Maggie was athletic and intelligent. The girls in her high school and in the neighborhood snubbed her so she hung around Burt. There were many times when she felt like the only one in the room. He became her best friend.

Large white pine trees glistened in the warm June sun most mornings, as far back as Maggie could remember.

Maggie and Burt's voices could be heard summer days over the lake as they competed with each other on who would row the boat or who swam the furthest on a particular day.

Burt and Maggie never minded working hard every summer picking pears, apples, blueberries and strawberries on the gentle rolling hills of East Jordan.

From Maggie's vantage point as a child, summer days in East Jordan were unforgettable. Growing up in a simpler time, feeling safe and sharing a strong bond with Burt, had sustained her throughout her life. Her father Sam, a widower, ensured she had everything she needed as a child from the loving family members that surrounded her.

Maggie remembered driving with Burt, slowly up a back road and looking out from an elevated bluff. Once there, she was transported to a beautiful retreat with its habitual forest, trout streams, islands, rivers, lakes, harbors, delicate sandy slopes and vastness of white pine trees.

Everything looked unusually beautiful, bright and new, just like they always looked when she was a child. She threw her head back with an infectious laugh, in spite of the cold and was happy of the wind on her face. The new green fresh leaves were blowing and flashing in the wind.

East Jordan[2] was located at the intersection of M-66 and M-32

---

2 The story of East Jordan began with Native Americans. "Bands of Ottawa Indians would encamp from time to time near the mouth of what is now the Jordan River."

where the famous Jordan River empties into the South Arm of Lake Charlevoix. It had a latitude of 45.1581 and longitude of 85.1241. It was on the same general latitude as northern Oregon and southern Maine.

Looking out from the top of a hill, one was lifted up from the humdrum of daily life to a peaceful vista, where clear blue shimmers of sky sifted through.

The East Jordan region was known for its many natural treasures. These included: Petoskey stones, a large variety of fish, wild fruits like plums and apples, Elm, ash, pine, cedar, hemlock, basswood, beech and maple trees, rivers and the chain of inland lakes throughout Antrim County.

Only thirteen miles from Charlevoix, the East Jordan River was given its name by Amos Williams[3] between 1840 and 1850.

---

3 "He was a religious man who imagined it resembled the Holy Land and gave the name "Jordan.""

CHAPTER 4

FALLING FROM GRACE
1940

Burt and Orville became fishing buddies or truth be told drinking buddies who fished. Burt recalled one day in the spring of 1940, when they were fishing near the shore of Lake Charlevoix in East Jordan and Burt wrapped his line around an electrical power line and simultaneously, the boat started moving from the wind. Burt, being stubborn, would not give up and the pole wire was taut.

"We better get out of here, Burt!" said Orville. Burt wasn't thinking clearly and got pulled into the water. He was thrashing around like a wounded manatee. Orville managed to get Burt back in the boat, up to the shore and led him to his car because he was unsteady on his feet. "Don't say a word Orville! Just take me home."

Burt made his way across town the next day to check out a job at Alan's grocery store and happened to run into Orville in the parking lot. "Money, money, money. Is that all you think about Burt?"

Burt took a deep breath.

"Listen up Orville, there are lots of guys working at the store and they are in competition with each other in tuna can stacking contests."

When he told him about it, Orville scoffed at Burt for not helping him clear away wild grape vines that grew along the driveway to his house, as he promised he would that day.

Burt just rolled his eyes.

Burt stomped out of the grocery store a few days later after work, and jumped into his 1938, green, Chevy truck. It was late spring, and one of the last suppers before summer vacation was to be held at the United Methodist Church on Fourth St. and Esterly at six o'clock. He hoped to run into Maggie. The church's white steeple could be seen from downtown. On a sign near the entrance were the words, "Faith, Hope, and Love. I Corinthians 13:13." Forsythias were in full bloom outside.

A few minutes later, Burt turned on his radio and calling out to him was Ricky Radio, WRAM double 009 on the AM dial. "All you bob bobber's better take heed. Storm clouds gathering over northern Michigan, so you better get off the lake!"

As Maggie turned into the long driveway at the Inn, a white sheet flew toward the car and covered the windshield. "This can't be good," she thought. Driving further down toward the Inn, she noticed the grass slope bespectacled with patches of white. At first, Maggie thought they were seagulls but, upon closer observation, she realized to her horror that the white spots were a sea of her undergarments.

Maggie parked her car and watched as one of her housekeeper's swished hither and thither chasing women's underwear, whitey tighties, sheets and pillowcases. Apparently, drying the laundry outside on the clothesline had backfired. The housekeepers warned her that a storm was brewing and it was a bad idea. Now, she had to agree. As they ran past her, with bundles of mud spattered and grass stained laundry in their arms, she couldn't look them in the eyes. "Well another idea gone with the wind," she observed.

News spreads fast in a small town and as Burt was driving home to change his clothes for the church supper, he heard Ricky Radio's voice, "That big storm just passed through and is headed toward Cheboygan with wind gusts up to 50 miles per hour. You ever heard the expression, 'it was raining cats and dogs?'"

"Well, today it was raining laundry. Whites to be specific. So if you listeners out there find a girdle or bra hanging from your weathervane, return it to Margaret Sanders at the Whispering Pines Inn. Tell her Ricky Radio sent you and be sure to have a piece of delicious homemade cherry pie!"

SUMMER OF 1940

The summer of 1940, Burt was 21 years old. His friend, Orville lived in the old Round Island Point Lighthouse that summer. Orville had a small yellow sailboat named Sunfish, and he gave the tourists sailboat rides around the Mackinac Island harbor. He was a tall and gawky fellow, with dark brown hair, brown eyes, freckles, a gap in front of his upper teeth and a quirky sense of humor.

Being 21 years old too, Orville was planning on going to the University of Michigan in the fall of 1940 and the money from his summer job was to cover his first semester. It being the 4th of July, Orville had the holiday off and decided to walk around the main street on the Island. The lighting in the Fudge Shop was dim. Orville noticed a cute girl working diligently making fudge. She wore a pink striped uniform and there was a strand of red hair hanging in her eyes that she kept blowing away from her face.

Kate was a local girl, meaning from East Jordan, and he realized that his venture into business as a sailboat skipper wasn't turning out as lucrative as he imagined it would. Kate got off work every night in a uniform covered with fudge. He had it all planned out—he would sail her over to the lighthouse for a barbeque and campfire dinner. He would cook beans and franks over the fire and gaze at the stars with Kate. He thought it a match made in heaven.

This was the first time they had been alone and they weren't aware of their surroundings until they suddenly realized it was now 10 P.M. and Lake Michigan was becalmed. No wind!

Orville knew he couldn't take Kate back at this point and put a green army blanket around her, saying, "I will flag down a passing speedboat." Kate smiled for the first time all night. She leaned her shoulder up against his and said, "I am fine right here."

By the end of the summer, Orville figured out that he didn't have the funds to go to U of M in the fall. He decided to follow Kate back to East Jordan and obtained a job at East Jordan Iron Works as a Journeyman machinist, making castings for machine parts, ships, agricultural parts and railroads. He was relieved that his life was moving in a positive direction. Orville could now say to his parents, who lived in Chicago, that he finally had a plan—he was going to be working hard at a good paying job and saving money for the next year. He ended up a foreman in later years.

Meanwhile, Kate contracted Scarlet Fever and was quarantined. She had been complaining of a sore throat, headaches, a rash on her neck, and a fever of 101 Fahrenheit. Orville went over to her house one blustery evening in September and saw the public health notice on the front door. He was absolutely confused. He went right home and telephoned Kate's house. Kate's father, John O'Hara explained the situation beautifully. His voice softened as he spoke, "Thank the good Lord that Kate is making progress every day and she is going to be alright."

Orville secretly wondered if her illness was his fault, thinking back to nights when they went out sailing on Lake Charlevoix and how the early autumn winds of Michigan caught them by surprise.

Orville was sleeping when his black Stromberg Carlson telephone rang two and half weeks later, and he heard Kate's voice. A spark had been ignited. The days Orville spent away from Kate made him understand clearly how deeply he loved her. It took a long time for Kate to fully recover and after the doctor said she would have a heart murmur for the rest of her life.

THE IRONTON FERRY & SHADES OF SUMMER 1940

Of Historic Note,
"Around 1876 passengers were for the first time able to ferry across the narrow South Arm of Pine Lake (Lake Charlevoix). The ferry owner and operator was Robert Bedwin, who also owned the Village Store and Village Post Office. It cost five cents a person to ride across in what was simply a row boat."
- *Historic Charlevoix* (Boyne City, Michigan: Harbor House Publishers, Inc., 1991), 42.

Burt recalled that with the advent of the automobile, traffic increased and a single cylinder engine was put in place to handle the load. Later years, the price of riding the ferry went up to 50 cents.

At the ripe old age of twenty-one, Burt took great pride in bragging to vacationers to the area how the Ferry acquired nationwide fame in 1936 when Ripley's Believe it or Not listed Ironton Ferry Captain, Sam Alexander as traveling 15,000 miles while never being more than ¼ mile from home[4].

Burt always felt a stir and a sense of excitement as he waited for Maggie and the Ironton Ferry.

Late in the day, there was a flicker of sun and shadow, as the waves lapped up against the shore. One particular Sunday night, in the summer of 1940, Burt took Maggie to the annual dance at the American Legion hall. As Burt held Maggie close, he felt intoxicated by the scent of Maggie's perfume on her neck and her body movement. He wanted to just stay right there all night long.

Burt often remembered standing with a camera slung over his shoulder near the dock, holding a bouquet of daisies, waiting for the Ironton Ferry to bring Maggie back from Boyne City. There was a spring in her step as she jumped out of her father's 1939 green Ford sedan and greeted him. Her father, Sam, wore horn-rimmed sunglasses and usually had a serious look on his face. He never had much to say. A yellow by-plane flew overhead.

Maggie whispered, "I'm half-starved so let's go get our teeth in some eats."

They got dropped off in downtown East Jordan and walked to a restaurant. They passed the beautiful Red Holly Hocks and Snow Ball Bushes that grew in front of porches and along narrow passageways between most any of the houses.

Burt was the tender hearted, sentimentalist in this relationship. Even with the ever-ready smile and always the jokester, Burt deep down inside was really the consummate romantic.

As time went by, he often went back in his mind to take a spiritual journey to a place far away—the deep dark lake gleaming in the moonlight, the sound of the wailing laugh of loons off in the distance, soft breezes, the clean, pine tree smell of northern Michigan air, the taste of fresh picked cherries and trout cooked over an open fire and summers that were all too brief.

CHAPTER 5

WORLD WAR II - BURT
1941

After the Japanese bombed Pearl Harbor, December 7, 1941, Burt decided to enlist in the Navy.

Maggie drove Burt to Charlevoix to see him off. Burt stood along the side of the white train depot holding Maggie's hand and for a fleeting moment, he managed to see beyond the surface of things. The spell of a crisp winter day, bursting with newly fallen snow fell over him and he just wanted to linger there with Maggie. Everything stood out; the bright blue sky, all the snow covered churches and houses that set this town apart from any other and the deep abiding love he felt for Maggie, his best friend. It was a world difficult to leave.

Every day Burt thought of the sultry, midsummer days he courted Maggie, long before the war tore them apart.

Burt remembered letters he wrote to Maggie while overseas:

March 10, 1942

Dear Maggie,

I miss you very much. It has only been a couple of months but I feel like it's been more like years.

I have always felt I could tell you anything. I hope you feel the same.

I just got into Saipan. Had a rough trip. It is beautiful here and warm today. Everywhere I go, I think of you. Please write very soon.

With love,

Burt

June 30, 1942

Dear Maggie,

Finally got some rest. There was a terrible storm here last night and our communications were down. The food doesn't compare with your homemade cooking. I was so happy to receive your letter and photograph today! You look pretty in your white crocheted blouse. I miss your smile and quirky sense of humor. I will write again soon.

All my love,

Burt

December 24, 1942

Dear Maggie,

We had lots of machinery trouble today.
Just have to get through it. I've made many
friends here. Did I mention Orville wrote to
me? He is planning to marry Kate soon. I will
never forget the story he told me about Kate
and how they met. I told him the days of tuna
can competitions were long behind us. Just
received your letter from August.

Everywhere I go, I see your face and
have to smile. Can't wait to receive your
next letter. I look forward to our future
Christmas's together and all the days and
nights thereafter.

Thinking of you on Christmas Eve and
sending wishes for a beautiful Christmas and
a Happy New Year.

With love,

Burt

January 25, 1943

Dear Maggie,

I don't understand why you don't write to
me. Is everything alright? I am so worried

about you. You know you can tell me anything.
It would mean the world to me if you could. I
have been assigned to the beach for the next
month. We have experienced heavy rainfall day
and night. The food is terrible.

Thinking of you as always,

Love,

Burt

Burt didn't hear from Maggie again.

What Burt didn't know at that time was Maggie had moved to Detroit during the war. She met Ted, a handsome young Airforce officer on leave before shipping out to England, married him and wept as he went off to war, just like so many other young brides. Confined to her small apartment that she shared with Norma, her friend and co-worker from Hudson's, she received the unbearable news that her husband died on a flight mission to Germany. Maggie was pregnant.

Maggie decided that the best thing to do would be to move back to East Jordan.

That evening, Reverend Polzin and his wife had Maggie and a few of her friends over to his house to tell her farewell, and led by the reverend, they knelt in prayer for the well-being of Maggie and her child. She never imagined the struggle would be either short or easy.

Her father helped her, along with loving friends until she could get back on her feet again.

Maggie gave birth to a healthy son, whom she named Harry on September 19, 1942.

The entire time Maggie lived in Detroit and thereafter, thoughts of Burt were never far away. Memories flooded her mind and images that should have been forgotten, were just beyond her grasp. Maggie knew she had to live up to her promise and commitment to Ted. Realizing he was a great man and although he was gone, she was mature enough and committed to raising their son, Harry, the way Ted would have wanted.

So Maggie didn't answer Burt's letters as her life took a completely different turn and the war progressed. She didn't want to give him false optimism and believed this was the right thing to do so Burt would stay focused on his responsibilities during his tour of duty.

As much as Maggie denied her heartfelt feelings for Burt, it wasn't the same for Burt. Burt was destined to become her lifelong friend and companion.

WORLD WAR II
1943

Burt's romantic endeavors had inevitably ended in disaster. His dealings with women were always clumsy but his efforts really ran amuck once Burt reached adulthood. In the spring of 1943, during his tour of duty in the Pacific, Burt met a young Filipino woman with a charismatic personality. He was somewhat infatuated with her. Her name was Petal and she worked as an aide to General Burke at the Filipino's consulate.

Petal was twenty-five years old, intelligent and very pretty.

Burt had been a Lieutenant in the Navy and was down in the radio room, listening to codes the Navy was intercepting. The Navy received intelligence from the Filipino resistance movement that they had captured a code that needed analysis. Burt was driven on a PT boat to the Philippines and immediately transported to the Filipino consulate. Petal acted as the liaison between Burt and the Filipino military. She was responsible for ensuring Burt had everything he needed to do his job. He was successful.

As overwhelming as it was to try to decipher the thousands of words and phrases in the Japanese naval codebook, Burt prevailed.

Petal initially looked after his welfare but after six months she truly began to understand what he was trying to accomplish and she feared she was in danger of being discovered. Petal was a spy for the Japanese.

In a strange twist of fate, Burt began looking at Petal with increasing suspicion, after witnessing evidence at hand that showed Petal had discharged an inquisitive Filipino military staff member. This discharge was malicious and without provocation. Burt read between the lines and could see she was a Japanese sympathizer.

Burt continued as the receiver who looked up each group in the corresponding code book and reassembled the message. The additional level of security added by enciphering the code groups was known as super enciphering. Petal's Japanese codes were intercepted by Naval intelligence and she was captured trying to escape.

The war raged on in Okinawa. It was May 8, 1945, and heavy Japanese fire and pouring rain kept the 7th Division from taking hill 187. One of Burt's old high school buddy's, Alfred, who was a soldier in the 7th Division, wrote to Burt about it. The battle in Okinawa lasted until June, 1945. Luckily, Burt's friend made it home.

By August 14, 1945, in the United States, the Armed Forces Radio Service beamed a command performance victory extra to the American Troops abroad. On August 25, 1945, Japan had surrendered. In London's Westminster Abby, the church bells pealed and a quarter of a million people surged before a balcony at Buckingham Palace, where the Royal family and Prime Minister

Churchill stood. People there and all over the world cheered. Bonfires burned all night in Hyde Park. Everyone watched rockets rise from Piccadilly Circus. All over the city search lights formed V's in the dark night sky. People could be heard singing, "God Save the King." It was hoped it meant the end of all wars.

Burt was given his discharge orders and after reporting to his superiors on his findings regarding Petal, he shipped out and returned to the states and eventually northern Michigan. His only thoughts on the plane home were, "Maggie's smile and had she ever thought of me over the past three years?" Burt wrote to Maggie six weeks earlier, informing her he was coming home soon.

Burt took the "Resort Special," a night train from Chicago to Charlevoix. All railroads were busy during World War II. He slept most of the trip, dreaming of Maggie and times they spent ice skating way out on frozen Lake Charlevoix a long time ago. Burt took Maggie's hand in his hand. He felt a strong north wind at his back and he moved easily across the ice and through the snow. He saw her beautiful glittering smile and dimples on her rosy cheeks so clearly. Her skates were always too small and then there was that unforgettable laugh. He would have followed her anywhere.

It was a cold morning when the train pulled into the station, and the locomotives belched magnificent clouds of steam onto the platform. As the gentle rolling motion of the train came to a halt, Burt slowly turned his head and looked out the window. There was no one waiting for him. He always held on to the hope in his heart that Maggie would be there. Burt sat with his shoulders slumped, and looked at the floor.

Burt stepped off the steps of the train onto the platform, down a few more steps, and then walked down the leaf-strewn sidewalk. He breathed in the scent of the sweet autumn air and was reminded of his boyhood days. Burt reached into his pocket and pulled out some loose change. He walked to the red telephone booth to call his old friend, Orville, to come and pick him up. He still held onto the dream of a new beginning and he hoped it was with Maggie.

CHAPTER 6

BURT RETURNS HOME
FALL 1945

Burt was tall in stature, with dark brown hair, bushy eyebrows and sparkling blue eyes.

Maggie always said when describing Burt to people, "He has a smile that lights up the room."

Burt's father, Edward wanted him to work the farm after he returned from his tour of duty. Instead, at the age of twenty-six, Burt went to the big city of Cheboygan to make his fame and fortune. He told his folks that he knew he had a tremendous opportunity in retail there. The truth was he didn't really know what he wanted to do with the rest of his life.

The third weekend in September, Burt's parents decided to drive all the way from East Jordan to Cheboygan to pay him a surprise visit. They packed a picnic lunch and a care package with some of Burt's favorite viands. They soon discovered to their dismay that he was employed as a bra fitter at Lane Bryant's. His proclamation to his parents was that Cheboygan offered him a tremendous business opportunity of which he just had to grab hold of.

His personal sales mantra was that a well-fitted brassiere was the foundation to success.

BULLET BRASSIERE

Brassieres looked like missile silos when Burt returned from the war.

Burt's father reflected, "Why all that time Burt spent at the East Jordan beach every summer wasn't wasted at all."

His parents soon discovered he was a gifted bra salesman. Burt whispered to the female bra fitter/sales clerk, "36CC, that's the ticket. Fit her with the Maidenform then sell her the Bali." The bottom dropped out of the brassiere market with the advent of the women's movement and Burt moved on to pantyhose. He sang the praises of the merits of pantyhose to any woman who would listen.

He was convincing too, as he preached how pantyhose could prevent varicose veins, make a woman's legs look incredible and keep you cool all day long.

BORED WITH BRAS

"Good Morning Burt," Sarah the sales clerk said. Burt looked back at her with a blank stare. It was the same lost look on his face as the one he had just before he went off to war.

"I am the butt of all the guys' jokes around town! I have submerged myself long enough in these bras! Besides, they remind me of the pyramids of Egypt."

This was around the time Burt decided to secure a job at the Inn and see Maggie again.

BURT MEETS HARRY
FALL 1945

The next day, Burt walked briskly up the stone walkway to Maggie's house on Kingsway Road. The two-story house had white shingles, a stone foundation, green and red stripped canvas awnings, and a large, old Birch tree in front with a sign her father put at the bottom that said, "East Jordan's Oldest Birch, Please Do Not Deface." A huge, oak tree stood off to the side of the house with spectacular colors of red and gold. Her father's 1944 black Ford was parked in the driveway.

Ruggedly handsome and with a serious demeanor, Burt knocked on the door. He focused his most careful attention on the familiar figure approaching from inside the darkened dining room. He heard loud noises in there, and glancing at the ground, saw a child's red wagon. In one corner of the porch sat a red tricycle. Maggie opened the door wide and with a look of anguish on her face, she ushered Burt inside.

"Welcome home stranger. I hope you will forgive my absence at the train depot," she said. She invited him to join her on the sofa. "There is so much to tell you, so much has happened. In good conscience I couldn't continue writing to you because of everything that took place in my life after the war began. You see, shortly after I moved to Detroit, I met an Airforce officer, whose name was Ted. We met at a Canteen in Detroit. He was a wonderful person, I think you would have really liked him Burt.

Well, we were in love and decided to get married. Shortly after, Ted shipped out. Two months later, I found out I was pregnant."

Burt was completely absorbed in everything Maggie had to tell him and fell silent.

Maggie continued, "You have to understand, I anguished over and over again about what to say to you, but couldn't come up with any answer that made sense at the time. I decided it best if I didn't write anymore and then you could stay focused on what you needed to do. My greatest concern at that time was my child and his welfare. I am so sorry Burt."

Soon after she poured out her heart to him, and told him how Ted died, Burt was greatly saddened but felt relief from a burden he'd been carrying for a long time. All along, he thought he had been responsible for something he didn't want to believe, the end of their love and friendship.

A couple of hours after Burt had found out the truth, he joined Harry in a game of hide and seek and as he hurried from hiding spot to hiding spot, Maggie, working in the kitchen, could hear their laughter coming from the living room. Suddenly the atmosphere in the house was full of sweetness and love. Burt smiled and knew he was finally home.

BURT AND HARRY
1948

One sunny, fall afternoon when Harry was six years old, Burt took him fishing. Shortly after noon, Burt patiently helped Harry bait his hook. Burt stood nearby and encouraged Harry to be still and wait calmly for a fish to jerk his line. Suddenly, the line moved up and down and Harry cried, "I've got one!"

Burt instructed him to keep holding the line steady while reeling him in. Burt's Golden retriever, Clancy barked loudly. Harry would always remember Burt's large, strong hands gently holding the fishing pole along with his and the sense of achievement he learned that day with Burt. He watched Burt in amazement as he slowly began to reel the bass in with care and precision. Harry wanted to stay longer, and shed a few tears over it, but the rustle of the wind in the trees and the fading of the late autumn sun told Burt it was time to go home. Burt had renewed faith now that there would be many more great moments with Harry like the one they shared today.

CHAPTER 7

BEGINNING OF RENOVATION
APRIL 1963

"It was the best of times, it was the worst of times."
- Charles Dickens

The sunlight poured through the three windows in Maggie's bedroom, and into her apartment situated off the back of the Inn.

Maggie stretched and yawned, and thought, "I guess I'm ready for what comes next."

She sat on the small chair with a peach colored seat, looked at herself in the three mirrors of the Mahogany dresser, brushed her long, auburn hair and pulled it back in a ponytail. Her hair had the beginnings of silver in it and her green and brown eyes showed signs of weariness.

Yellow curtains hung on the windows with tie backs. Overgrown moss and ivy made its way up the outside of the Inn. Brimming with confidence, Maggie's strategy was to head over to her office and start to go through the mail.

The day began with Maggie looking out past the lobby, through the restaurant's windows out to the lake. The chilly April weekday showed no signs of improving. A heavy mist still blanketed Lake Charlevoix and the expanse of grass which went down to the lake.

Maggie glanced at the clock, "Well, now or never," she thought. She stretched and cinched up her bedraggled pink robe. She put on an old second-hand knee length blue wool coat, slipped into her Sorel boots, and found her canvas beige hat. Maggie opened the office back door and braced herself as the reality of a cold damp April morning in Northern Michigan greeted her and sent a shiver down her spine.

Maggie plunged forth across the parking lot and schlepped up the mid snow covered ground to the main East Jordan throughway, two lane road. Reaching the main road, Maggie pulled the Traverse City Record Bulldog from its box, at the side of the mailbox. She scanned the headlines, then herself.

Her April ensemble was warm and practical yet still preposterous.

"And why don't I ever get selected for the Annual East Jordan Chamber of Commerce Fashion Show I'll never know," she said to herself.

Maggie began the slow trek back down the sloping gravel road to the Whispering Pines Inn. Large patches of snow still covered the grounds. She stopped halfway, and surveyed her domain. Harry was picking up deadfalls and what autumn leaves he could reach. He was going to be putting the dock in the water soon. Maggie stumbled to where the staff were beginning their day.

The cook stood out back smoking probably his sixteenth of the day. The young housekeeper, Roberta puffed away, at methodically deep cleaning each guest room for the summer season. Roberta was an innately talented but untrained potter and was beginning to sell her work at a couple of the local art galleries in East Jordan.

"My crack team, a rag-tag bunch of ineffectual forces at work," Maggie sarcastically thought.

"And me, in charge of it all. Well, another day, another debt," she ruminated, shaking her head in disbelief. She shook the mist from her shoulders like an old Labrador and returned to her office.

BURT REMINISCES ABOUT THE GOOD OLD DAYS & SMELT DIPPING 1963

Of Historic note-"Rainbow smelt are native to lakes and streams along both the Pacific and Atlantic coasts of North America. They can live in both saltwater and freshwater. They have spread or were introduced to lakes across the U.S. and are found in all five Great Lakes. They are 7-9 inches in length and weigh 3 ounces."

-Martha Thierry, Rainbow Smelt (Sea Grant Minnesota: Detroit Free Press., U.S. Geological Survey, 2015)

Burt called a truce. The balky old green Studebaker refused to start and Burt's diagnostic skills were simply not up to the task of solving its problem at that moment. He was stubborn enough not to give up but smart enough to realize when he needed a break, so he wiped his greasy hands on a rag, walked out of the mechanics work shed, and gazed down toward Lake Charlevoix[5]. At the Inn, Maggie was in a similar predicament. The ongoing trapeze act of

---

5 "Lake Charlevoix also located in Charlevoix County is big water. Back in the 1950s it was gaining a large following of smelt anglers from all over Michigan and the Midwest. Highlighted many times in the early years of Mort Neff's television show "Michigan Outdoors," it hosted several large villages of ice shanties on the north and largest arm of the lake. Today only local anglers go out in the evening for smelt on a regular basis. The fishery and smelt are still there for those who know about it."

deciding which bills to pay and which to delay was, at the moment, beyond her grasp. She welcomed the interruption when Burt stepped into the office and plopped into a chair.

Soon the conversation turned to the good old days. To Burt, the good old days meant fond memories of fishing and hunting. It being April, his thoughts turned to smelt[6] dipping. "It used to be that you could fill a minnow bucket with smelt[6] with one dip of the net when they were running upstream from the big lake. Not anymore," Burt bemoaned.

"Isn't that the truth?" Maggie agreed.

"That's not to say you were always guaranteed success," Burt continued. "On the best smelt streams you had to stake your spot near the stream mouth early in the evening or you were out of luck. And too often some yahoos would make a commotion and scare off the smelt. They won't run when suckers are running and sometimes they wouldn't run up a stream at all."

Burt continued to reminisce. "I remember one time my father got the inside scoop on a little smelt stream off of the South Arm of Lake Charlevoix. We got there just after dusk. The only other dippers were a big family from Paradise Valley, over Alba way. Well sure enough, the fish started running heavy about nine o'clock but they weren't smelt, just suckers. We were disappointed but the Alba

---

6 "Smelt have been a popular sport fish in Michigan since the early 1900s. But East Jordan residents gave this diminutive species special recognition when, on March 9, 1932, they organized the 'National Order of Smelt.' The next year, Lewis Cornell, secretary of the East Jordan Chamber of Commerce, stated, 'Can't we stage some kind of celebration during the peak of the smelt run?' It was decided that crowning a 'Smelt Queen' would be too much like other communities. Why not do something more original? The idea emerged to crown a king instead, serve a stag banquet and make it a real he-man affair. The concept was accepted and on March 18, 1933, the first East Jordan National Smelt Jamboree was held. Al Warda, a retired vaudeville actor living near East Jordan was crowned 'Albert I, King of Smeltium.'"

family was ecstatic; that's what they'd come for. My father had no inclination whatsoever to dip for a lousy sucker. I was about 11 years old. Seeing that I didn't particularly care what kind of fish I caught, he took up the Alba family's offer to babysit me and promptly departed for destinations unknown.

I was a mite dismayed at the turn of events which the evening had taken. Early on, well before my father left, I sensed that the Alba brood was cut from a different cloth or, as their Granpappy Roscoe would have said, "We don't chew the same brand of tobaccy." There were a few red flags. The men folk all wore bib overalls with a hip flask accoutrement. Fish catching paraphernalia included spears, gaffs, clubs, rakes and a BB gun. Not a single legitimate smelt dipping net could be found among them.

When the suckers started running, the family waited patiently. Several family members blocked the suckers' progress upstream with a couple of strategically placed aluminum garbage cans.

Suckers continued running up the stream and soon they schooled in deep pools, backed up like rush hour on the Motor City's John C. Lodge Freeway. "OK boys, let's get at it," Grandpa declared. His command was greeted with a rousing crescendo of war whoops, as the Alba clan descended on the stream to wreak havoc on the sucker run. A methodical delegation of authority soon became apparent. Fishers caught the suckers by hook or crook and tossed them on the stream bank. Stevedores deposited the fish in buckets and boxes which teamsters transported to the bed of a pickup truck. The work continued for hours.

I contributed as best I could. With a little pan fish net, I was able to dip a modest number of fish. "He don't get too many but what he gets are biguns," one man observed.

"I think we just trained ourselves a sucker dipper," his wife chimed in. Everyone laughed and I laughed along with them. The suckers were to be driven home and stored overnight in a cool water well pool. Next morning began the tedious, careful process of cleaning the fish and canning them in a brine of apple cider vinegar, salt and sugar. The canned suckers, along with venison, would provide an important source of protein for the family well into the next spring."

CHAPTER 8

BOB BUYS A BARBERSHOP
APRIL 1963

Bob Thibodeau was a black man. If most anyone were asked to describe him, that's the description they would give. Mr. Thibodeau was also a nose tackle for the LSU football team, an artilleryman in the Korean War, an injured vet with shrapnel still embedded in his right thigh, a skilled mechanic, a widower with grown children and grandchildren and a transplanted Southerner whose family moved north to work at the Ford Rouge plant in Dearborn Michigan. But if you were to ask Bob Thibodeau to describe himself, he would, like a majority of men, identify himself by profession.

"I'm a barber. I own my own shop on Dexter Ave., Detroit," he would proudly say.

Bob Thibodeau went to Detroit Barber College, got his first job at that very barbershop on Dexter and eventually bought out its owner.

Bob liked cutting hair. No two heads were the same. No two people were the same. He liked his shop when it was bustling. He liked his shop when it was quiet. He particularly liked the camaraderie. Guys coming in just to pass the time of day. But in the late 1950s, white flight had just started to take its toll. His stable, integrated west side neighborhood had changed. There was a tension in the air. Bob heard stories. He started carrying a pistol to work.

Soon Bob found himself reading the "Business for Sale" section of the Barber News want ads. Casually, at first, but soon in earnest.

"Just swap out the barbershop on Dexter for a shop in a little town somewhere. Peace and quiet. A place in the sun," Bob dreamed.

Months of searching ended in frustration. The few leads he found were dead ends.

A persistent man, Mr. Thibodeau revised his search strategy and started visiting the main branch of the Detroit Public Library on Woodward Avenue, perusing the want ads of mid-sized Michigan towns. And there he found it:

> *Barbershop 4 Sale, E. Jordan, MI*
> *Turnkey business; must sacrifice*
> *Contact Hertler Realty*

Bob made the call, took a whirlwind one-day visit and did the deal. He would have to worry about selling the Dexter shop in the near future but he had barbers ready to take up the slack. When he broke the news to his regulars, a group of retired political pundits and social commentators who had been hanging around the barbershop for almost a decade, the response was not encouraging.

"East Jordan! Where the hell is East Jordan?"

"Oh no! You done stepped in it now."

"Is there some way you can get out of it? Maybe plead temporary insanity."

"I hear tell the Central Lake Historical Museum has a KKK

robe displayed in its little log cabin. It's part of its heritage. Welcome to the neighborhood."

"Man, all you had to do when you was up there was count the number of brothers you saw. Did you see any? Any?"

Bob's dream of a place in the sun did not seem so sunny anymore.

"They gonna think you can only cut Black hair. What'cha goin' to do then?"

THE CHAT AND CHEW CAFÉ
APRIL 1963

The best way to start the day in this neck of the woods was with a good early breakfast. You could clear away the cobwebs with the strong coffee served at the Chat and Chew Café, or as some of the people in a slump like to call it, the Scratch and Screw.

The following Tuesday, Maggie met her Coffee Clutch at the Chat and Chew. Tucked away on Maple Street, the restaurant was known for its friendly atmosphere, generous servings and home-cooked meals. Maggie knew that just because there was a lack of pretentiousness, it didn't mean the folks frequenting it were lacking in manners or culture. What she needed was a strong cup of coffee and a good dose of gossip. The Chat and Chew served up both.

Maggie joined a group of women ensconced in a corner booth, and with coffee served, began to catch up. The talk wound around to new, then faults and then lack of redeeming qualities.

"How's that General Manager working for you?" A friend asked inquisitively, amid titters.

As Maggie struggled for an answer, her attention was diverted to the front door of the Café. Burt walked in and plopped on a red vinyl stool at the lunch counter. Maggie turned her back to her inquisitors in silence.

"Well, I guess that answers that question."

Back at the lunch counter, Burt ordered biscuits and gravy. He sloshed down a couple cups of black coffee, seemingly oblivious to the presence of Maggie, just a few tables away.

Back at the booth, Maggie's friend Iris asked, "How did the Inn hold up when that big storm blew through?" More giggles.

Maggie slammed her coffee cup down on the table, regained her composure and answered, "Roof damage. We had leaks in two guest rooms."

Burt devoured his breakfast quickly and pulled out a thin book with a blue cloth cover. "What are you reading?" Eleanor, the owner asked.

"Keats," Burt answered.

"You read John Keats?" Maggie inquired from her booth. "I love Keats."

Without further encouragement Burt flipped to "*A Thing of Beauty is a Joy Forever*" and began reading out loud.

A thing of beauty is a joy for ever:
Its loveliness increases; it will never
Pass into nothingness; but still will keep
A bower quiet for us, and a sleep
Full of sweet dreams, and health, and quiet breathing.
Therefore, on every morrow, are we wreathing
A flowery band to bind us to the earth,
Spite of despondence, of the inhuman dearth
Of noble natures, of the gloomy days,
Of all the unhealthy and o'er-darkened ways
Made for our searching: yes, in spite of all,

At first his recitation was directed toward Eleanor, but as he continued reading, his voice rose.

> *Some shape of beauty moves away the pall*
> *From our dark spirits. Such the sun, the moon,*
> *Trees old, and young, sprouting a shady boon*
> *For simple sheep; and such are daffodils*
> *With the green world they line in; and clear rills*
> *That for themselves a cooling covert make*
> *'Gainst the hot season; the mid-forest brake,*
> *Rich with a sprinkling of fair musk-rose blooms:*
> *And such too is the grandeur of the dooms*
> *We have imagined for the mighty dead;*
> *All lovely tales that we have heard or read:*
> *An endless fountain of immortal drink,*
> *Pouring unto us from the heaven's brink.*

As the poem took over his emotions, he stood up and addressed the masses.

> *Nor do we merely feel these essences*
> *For one short hour; no, even as the trees*
> *That whisper round a temple become soon*
> *Dear as the temple's self, so does the moon,*
> *The passion poesy, glories infinite,*
> *Haunt us till they become a cheering light*
> *Unto our souls, and bound to us so fast*
> *That, whether there be shine or gloom o'ercast,*
> *They always must be with us, or we die.*

The Chat and Chew fell silent. The inaugural poetry slam at the

Chat and Chew mesmerized the audience.

> *Therefore, 'tis with full happiness that I*
> *Will trace the story of Endymion.*
> *The very music of the name has gone*
> *Into my being, and each pleasant scene*
> *Is growing fresh before me as the green*
> *Of our own valleys: so I will begin*
> *Now while I cannot hear the city's din;*
> *Now while the early budders are just new,*
> *And run in mazes of the youngest hue*
> *About old forests; while the willow trails*
> *Its delicate amber; and the dairy pails*
> *Bring home increase of milk. And, as the year*
> *Grows lush in juicy stalks, I'll smoothly steer*
> *My little boat, for many quiet hours,*
> *With streams that deepen freshly into bowers.*

He walked up one aisle and down the other, his voice quivering with emotion upon reading the final stanza.

> *Many and many a verse I hope to write,*
> *Before the daisies, vermeil rimmed and white,*
> *Hide in deep herbage; and ere yet the bees*
> *Hum about globes of clover and sweet peas,*
> *I must be near the middle of my story.*
> *O may no wintry season, bare and hoary,*
> *See it half finished: but let Autumn bold,*
> *With universal tinge of sober gold,*
> *Be all about me when I make an end!*
> *And now at once, adventuresome, I send*
> *My herald thought into a wilderness:*

There let its trumpet blow, and quickly dress
My uncertain path with green, that I may speed
Easily onward, thorough flowers and weed.

-*John Keats*

Burt came to a stop at Maggie's booth and as the poem came to its conclusion, he looked straight into her eyes. Tears streamed down her face. "Please, Please, Please" by James Brown could be heard playing in the background on the Wurlitzer juke box.

He closed the book, and walked out the door.

"Hey, what about the bill?" Maggie exclaimed.

Maggie pulled out a hanky to dry her eyes, cleared her throat, and entered the ladies bathroom. As she was about to exit, she noticed a card on the counter that said, "If you notice an issue in this bathroom just give this to the owner. No words needed."

She sighed, and thought to herself, "I feel the same way about Burt and his poem, no words needed."

ROSALIE
SPRING 1963

That spring, the circus came to town in East Jordan. This was an annual event and the locals always had a renewed interest in it. They were glad to see it go when it was over, but by the time the New Year came, they forgot all the previous year's shenanigans.

During the early 1960's, Burt hung out most mornings at the Chat and Chew Café. One particular morning in late April, Burt noticed a lady sitting in a booth, who was the ticket taker at the circus that had already left. He noticed her there every day for over a week. She seemed heartbroken by the downcast look she had. Burt got up his nerve to talk to her and within five minutes, she was pouring out her heart to him. Her name was Rosalie. She was the girlfriend of the Lion and Elephant trainer but time waits for no one and she lost her good looks and had outgrown her usefulness.

Burt took Rosalie over to the Inn and introduced her to Maggie. That was how Rosalie came to live there. She had a large, black humpback traveling chest and stacks of circus posters. That was the extent of her possessions. Inside of the chest was a khaki uniform with epaulets, a clown outfit and a magician's assistant sequined leotard. Louie, who was hired to assist Burt with maintenance problems at the Inn, told Maggie that the new resident, Rosalie, was dressing weird. Maggie replied, "Would you rather have her dress weird or act weird?" Maggie continued, "Sounds to me like she's fitting right in."

BOB CONNECTS WITH THE LOCALS-LATE APRIL 1963

Bob looked up at the clock on the green wall of his new barbershop. It was lunchtime. He folded up his Detroit Free Press, took off his black smock and washed his hands. He took a five-dollar bill from the cash drawer.

"One haircut, all morning, one haircut. Enough for a hearty lunch, tax, tip and change leftover. Top King of the world," he sardonically observed.

Bob put on his coat and hat. He slipped out of his loafers and into a new pair of Sorel winter boots, fleece long extra. A glance in the mirror revealed a deranged black Michelin man.

"Well, time for a little community outreach. Press the flesh, work the room," he thought.

He put the "gone to lunch" sign on the door and set the cardboard clock hands for one o'clock. Bob opened the barbershop door, bracing himself for the bitter, twenty-five mile per hour wind coming off the remaining ice at the top of the south arm of Lake Charlevoix. He headed down the street toward the Chat and Chew Café. Already, he could see that the cooking and crowd of lunch patrons had steamed up the cafés front windows. He stepped off the sidewalk, straight down into a six inch puddle of icy slush. The Sorel's kept his feet dry and warm.

"Well, least I got a good pair of boots out of this whole mess." He crossed the street and entered the Café. He hoped to slip into the back booth, eat a hungry man breakfast platter, and go back to the shop. The place was packed. The lunch counter, center row of Formica tables and booths were all occupied. He stood there like a fool, self-conscious. He felt all eyes on him, then, from the back two taps, by the kitchen door, he saw that woman...the one who dressed oddly and had accosted him on the street...waving to him, motioning him to join her. He hesitated. She pushed her chair back, ready to get up and confront him with a formal invitation.

"Too late to flee, better to cut my losses at this point," he whispered.

"Shouldn't you be getting back for the afternoon rush?" she asked.

"If she wanted to know how business was, this was certainly a unique way to find out," he muttered to himself.

"No, no afternoon rush," he replied.

"Business slow this time of the year?" she inquired, as if she didn't know that, essentially, he had no business. "Slow," he answered politely.

"Well, you know," she began.

"Here it comes," he thought.

"Everybody's a business expert. Everybody's got an opinion," she said.

"Here it comes, what's it gonna be," Bob thought.

"Just thought I would mention that Burt Armstrong, over at the Whispering Pines Inn, is looking for a qualified and experienced mechanic. You might want to check it out," said Rosalie.

Burt met Bob the next day at the Chat and Chew, felt comfortable with him and worked to dispel Bob's anxiety. Burt was impressed with Bob's overall demeanor and new Sorel's.

"Listen man, I promise you will have a job at the Inn anytime you say the word."

"I need a responsible mechanic!"

"Besides, Louie's nature being what it is, I need someone who is reliable," said Burt.

Burt recognized a man who had an innate sense of knowledge when it came to fixing things. For the first time, Bob decided to follow a path of courage, not fall prey to appeasement.

CLEAR THE DECKS
APRIL 1963

Maggie told Burt to start clearing debris out one section at a time. He began by going room to room. Burt tried not to seem too eager. Burt checked the foundation and the roof first. Next, he cleaned out all the pipes and checked all of the voltage systems. He found that the roof had a leak, from observing the water stains on the pine paneling in the lobby. He decided to save Maggie some money and reverse the paneling. The furnace was temperamental. Burt replaced the pilot, and upgraded the room thermostats. One toilet on the second floor, fell through to the room below. Burt called Bob for assistance.

Just to keep Louie out of his way, he gave him the assignment of "inspecting the garden." Burt told him, "Report back to me later."

It being Saturday, Louie asked if he could get overtime pay. Burt just gave him a "look" that said, "Go away."

"There is a lot of furniture," Burt told Maggie. "I expected this," Maggie responded. There was a gay couple who lived in town and they came by the Inn every other night to see what was thrown out. One guy ran the Pick and Choose Consignment store in town. Burt started a rumor at the Chat and Chew Café, "Look I'm an expert on decorating!" He slowly started becoming an annoying know-it-all.

Maggie started every day by putting things out for the Salvation Army to pick up near the road. Burt, in turn, put it back every day into a storage room on the second floor of the Inn. This went on for a week. One day Maggie opened the door to the storage room and soon discovered Burt had retrieved all the furniture and old items she threw out. She sat down clumsily in a brown overstuffed chair and sighed a big sigh of defeat. She had a bottle of Robert Mondavi Red and a glass with her because she was going to put it in the wine cellar. Now she opened it and by the second glass, her situation did not seem so mind-boggling.

A little while later, she made an executive decision to throw all items out the second floor window and wash her hands of the faded, dusty furniture and stuffed animal heads. Burt, working outside, ran to see what all the racket was about and found a heap of broken furniture on the lawn. A deer head with antlers flew out of the window, crashing at his feet. "Ah, she must be in the antler suite!" Burt mused to himself. The cheap old desk hit the ground, breaking up, and Burt found what appeared to be Hemingway memorabilia.

There were train tickets, notebook ideas, notes, and an uncompleted manuscript dated November 1921 that belonged to Hemingway, written by him to his girlfriend. He also found a restaurant menu, a playbill, and a music festival program from the Fair View Association in Petoskey. Burt was ecstatic with the find.

The memorabilia was wrapped up in an old faded, men's shirt with a silk ribbon around it, but Maggie was ready to move on. She gathered it all up to take to the local historian at the Historical Society in Charlevoix for verification, knowing it could be very valuable.

The following day, Maggie heard a knock at the front door. "How do you do Miss Sanders, my name is James Lawrence and I am a reporter from the Traverse City Record Beagle Newspaper. Would you mind me interviewing you for an article on the Hemingway memorabilia?"

She told him everything she knew about the material, Hemingway papers, and his connection with the Inn. Mr. Lawrence took her picture and one of the Inn before thanking her profusely and promising a front-page story.

The interview had taken an hour. As soon as the door closed behind the reporter, Maggie flopped into her comfortable, green winged-back chair by the window in her office. She smiled, thinking, "I guess it is never too late to become a celebrity, and the publicity from this can't hurt the Inn!"

Over time, Maggie sold most of the other items at Auction in New York City at Sotheby's. She kept a few things such as a number of letters, and a bracelet with an engraving on it. Maggie created a display case in the front lobby with these items in it and a sign that said, "Hemingway slept here."

CHAPTER 9

MADAME ZOSHIA
1963

It was early May, 1963 and Maggie was sitting on the screened porch that faced the lake, sipping a glass of iced tea. She glanced at the thermostat and at 9:00 A.M. it was already 75 degrees.

"I just have to go up into the attic today, find that old Sears electric window fan and persuade Burt to install it for me," she thought.

Maggie raced to her office to start tackling her paperwork, when suddenly, she noticed a red and white, 1956 DeSoto station wagon come to a full stop near the door. That automobile was intended for more than just driving.

Once the dust settled, a well-dressed woman[7] approached Mag-

---

7 "Most Horton Bay people made a point of being friendly and hospitable, but in the first 20 years of this century, once or twice a summer a band of gypsies came through town, and I remember distinctly that they were never welcome; were in fact, feared. Before cars were common, they showed up in horse-drawn wagons of considerable size, not unlike the Conestoga wagons that blazed trails out west. These vehicles were full of grown gypsies and numerous little gypsies, both sexes, jeweled and bespangled, gaily dressed in bright yellows and reds and

gie as she entered the office. The woman wore beige linen slacks, and a crisp white shirt rakishly unbuttoned. Her dark brown hair was stylishly coiffed in a flip. Maggie picked up a sense of urgency from the woman.

"Good morning, miss," the woman said.

"Good morning, how can I help you?" Maggie said leading her to an antique Windsor back chair.

The woman introduced herself, "My name is Zoshia Riddle."

"I need to rent a place for at least three months," she said.

"I have rooms, cabins, and detached cottages," said Maggie.

Sitting on the edge of the chair, the woman asked, "Is there a lease?"

"No," Maggie replied.

"I plan to stay for an extended period but my employment demands that I be able to leave at a moment's notice," countered the prospective guest.

Maggie looked at Zoshia, who was spellbound, and cleared her throat.

"Your timing is perfect, because I happen to have a clean, updated cottage all ready for you to move in to."

The new guest wasted no time telling Maggie, "I consider a cottage an oasis of tranquility, a rustic retreat from the "cark an' care" of modern life, an escape to a quieter time."

Everything seemed fine and she paid cash in advance.

Maggie thought to herself, "Wow, this could turn into a long

---

greens and blues, and sporting big silver and gold ear-rings. Their big wagons seemed to be stuffed with all their earthly possessions, and whatever couldn't be stowed inside hung on the outside. They were crammed to the nines with water barrels, dangling tinware, hand tools, small trunks, camping gear, and drying laundry waving in the breeze. In later years, their caravans were made up of very large touring cars but their routine was always the same when they stopped in Horton Bay. I never knew what the commotion was all about. None of my friends turned up missing, but the panic when the gypsies came was very real."

term deal!" Maggie was impressed by Miss Riddle's demeanor and was anxious to accommodate her. Maggie thought nothing unusual about her next question, "Is there zoning in effect in this township?"

"She's just quirky. I can live with quirky," Maggie thought to herself. Maggie opened the large pine box on the wall and reached for the key to the cottage. Smiling and handing the key to her, Maggie was undeterred by the zoning question again.

To be polite, Maggie excused herself and pressed ahead through a stack of bills. On the way out the door Zoshia said, "I can really get down to business tomorrow!"

The next day, Maggie saw a swarthy guy with a U-Haul trailer moving a few pieces of furniture into the new guests' cottage. Maggie thought, "Holy Cow, she really plans on staying for the duration and I may have a long term resident here. And to top it off she is so charming!"

Just one problem – Maggie wasn't aware of Zoshia's hidden agenda for coming to stay in the small town and at the Inn.

HARRY

Harry sometimes wondered if he was missing something, having lived his entire life in a remote and rather secluded part of northern Michigan. Burt, Maggie, and his grandfather, Sam always told Harry, "God was looking out for him," and he was thankful for the early life he had. Still, he thought, "What do I know of the rest of the world?"

Harry was what you would call a naturalist. He had worked as a fishing guide, a cross-country trail groomer and had some experience mole hunting. Roberta enjoyed looking into Harry's blue eyes, and sharing his company. Harry, was devoted to his mother, Maggie, and was responsible for gardening, landscaping and general outside maintenance of the Inn. Harry was tall, with short blondish brown hair, trim and most days liked to wear oxford shirts with combed cotton slacks.

Harry had a great sense of humor, just like his mother, but being only 22 years old, was self-absorbed most of the time.

His mother often found him lying in a hammock, which he referred to as "his office." He liked to think of himself as a "jack-of-all-trades."

Harry was so easily distracted by Roberta that it was an ordeal to keep him on task. Thus, he was always bumping into things. Who wouldn't be, with those blue eyes, blue mascara, brown hair and bright smile?

Harry enjoyed taking the Inn guests on canoe trips and city slickers frequently asked, "Which end is the front?" to which he gave a polite but bemused response, "The front end."

Maggie had learned over time that Harry had to be given specific instructions on a daily basis.

Harry introduced an idea to Maggie for the avid fly fishermen who came to stay at the Inn in the spring. He thought it would be great fun to post a tradition that said, "The guys in even numbered rooms shall wear paisley shirts on Tuesdays and the guys in odd numbered rooms shall wear madras shirts on Thursdays." Maggie agreed and said, "Harry go now and spread the word like horse manure."

CHEF CLAUDE
1963

Maggie hired a Chef for the summer. Intuition told her to hire him. He was a French trained Chef from Lyons France named

Claude. He had lost many jobs due to his drinking. Claude was 53 years old now and had a potbelly, red nose and cheeks due to a long history of drinking. He had a temper when he was younger and high standards that he held others to, but not himself. Claude was a stocky guy with dark brown hair, a receding hairline, large ears, tortoiseshell brow line glasses, brown eyes and a broad smile.

Early in May, Maggie showed up in his kitchen and tormented Chef by trying to get him to include oleo, bouillon cubes and margarine in his recipes, but he was not having any of it.

Chef tried new dishes that nobody wanted but he realized he was just calling them a wrong name. He had a little black dog (chi Wawa and terrier mix) that barked a lot. The dog's name was Buddy.

One warm day in May, Buddy got loose and he was later found at the Inn's main parking lot, barking like crazy and running back and forth.

By now, a few of the guests were alerted by the barking and asked each other where Buddy was. Some of the guests knew Buddy was an inveterate crotch sniffer and they would not be sad if he disappeared. Most of the locals just thought of him as a minor annoyance. Suddenly, Buddy showed up and the dog underwent an amazing transformation. He strolled indignantly towards his master and leaped into his arms. He gave him a wet kiss on the cheek and burrowed into the safety of Claude's elbow.

Then he gave one final parting growl to the bystanders in the parking lot.

Chef Claude himself viewed the crowd with disdain and with a shake of his head turned on his heels and marched off.

One local observed, "Well there goes my musky bait."

CHOUCROUTE

Sally, the Chef's assistant, had sniffles but she had her orders.

"Tonight, the Chef especially made a Choucroute. I recommend it."

The three generations of German cattle farmers, all eight hungry customers looked at her in dismay. "Shot curd. Doesn't sound appetizing to me," Ronnie the son-in-law proclaimed.

No one laughed.

"What's a shot curd?" Grandma asked.

Sally struggled to find her notes. "Its sauerkraut and pork," she replied.

"What kind of pork?" Grandma inquired.

"Just a minute." Sally went to the kitchen and quickly reappeared with a soup bowl of Choucroute and a handful of spoons. Chef had specifically told her to push the envelope.

"A sample from the Chef. It's got bratwurst, knockwurst, ham hocks and a chunk of ham, and if you like, a fritter." Grandpa smacked his lips and ordered the Choucroute. The others chimed in. Sally smiled.

"May I bring this out family style? A big pot. Then everyone can pick what they want. There will be plenty for everyone, and if not, I can bring some more," Sally said.

"That sounds great," Ronnie's spouse declared.

Sally returned to the kitchen to place the order. Chef, encouraged by the first Choucroute order of the season, cracked open the kitchen door and took a peek at his customers delight and grinned.

"He's a big cattle and pig farmer, very successful. Tell him I wish to speak to him after dinner," Chef said.

"Sure," Sally said shrugging her shoulders.

The contented family made a halfhearted attempt at seconds

without much success. The dinner was finished off with lemon meringue pie and coffee. There were big smiles all around.

"Chef wishes to speak to you," Sally told the grandfather.

"Well okay," he answered. Grandpa followed Sally into the kitchen. The conversation was brief.

As the grandfather returned to his family, Sally caught up to Chef.

"What was that all about?" Sally inquired.

"I'm going on a tour of a hog and cattle farm tomorrow," Chef answered.

TROUBLE WITH NANCY
MAY 1963

Maggie sat in the green, worn wing back chair, sipped her Lipton iced tea and read the Traverse City Record Beagle News, which she enjoyed for its vast coverage of local crimes and misdemeanors. Nancy thought nothing of just showing up at Maggie's office early that morning with curlers still in her hair. "There's a lot of traffic at Zoshia's!" said Nancy. To be polite, she escorted Nancy to the office door and simply excused herself with the words, "Good, good and I will certainly follow up on your concerns, but I must leave you now because the roof repairman is scheduled to be here at any moment." She glared at Nancy, who was now leaving her office. At first, Maggie didn't want to believe Nancy's accusations about Zoshia. Then, employees of the bank where Maggie had her accounts started asking her, "Where is Miss Riddle from and what business is she in?"

Next, one of the bankers who knew Maggie personally asked her with one raised eyebrow, "Why is Miss Riddle interested in bearer bonds?" Maggie perked up and said, "It's a mystery to me

Carl. Gotta go for now, lots to do at the Inn."

Maggie found out that day that her new guest was conducting business with three different banks in East Jordan. As Maggie headed for the front door at her bank, clerks emerged from their desks and said, "Thanks Maggie for all of the business from Miss Riddle!" Maggie dashed out the door.

She got in her car and fought back tears. Maggie took little solace in the knowledge that she was the sole orchestrator of this fiasco.

Nancy moved into one of the cottages at the same time Zoshia moved in and paid three months' rent in advance. Maggie was ecstatic about this considering all the bills that were mounting up.

The only problem was Nancy thought she had a lot of authority now. Nancy made lots of complaints, i.e. the birds chirped too much, a bird pooped on her windshield, a squirrel peeped in her window, the lake was too cold, the water tasted funny, the sun was too hot, it was too windy, the loons were too loud, the lawnmower woke her up, the moles were digging holes in her flower pots and leaving messes, Charlevoix was too far away and no one was monitoring the parking lot so she never had the same parking spot.

She had an umbrella clothes hanger outside of her cottage. Nancy always hung her clothes out to dry on it. Being 5 feet tall, the umbrella clothes hanger proved to be less of a challenge than the close line. Nancy wore the same boring clothes, year in and year out such as beige or black Bermuda shorts or slacks, white cotton sleeveless shirts, jeans that didn't fit properly and beige Vintage Dancer shoes with laces. She was always running down to the Rexall Drug store to buy new Maybelline eyebrow pencils. Her eyebrows were quite exaggerated but she thought they looked natural. They certainly got her noticed and remembered by the locals and even on a calm and sunny day, those high eyebrows had a haunted look.

It was an unusually busy Thursday afternoon and Louie was pressed for time.

Louie found himself facing a lawnmower crisis. His solution, cut up Nancy's Playtex bra to use as an emergency fan belt for the lawnmower. Suddenly it blew off.

"What to do, what to do," cried Louie.

Louie hid the damaged evidence of his petty offense in a trash receptacle in back of Nancy's cottage.

Friday morning arrived hot and humid and after getting all of her groceries put away, Nancy headed over to the Maggie's office. Louie sat in an old desk chair with wheels on it, spun around, and waited patiently for Maggie to give him his work orders for the day. Burt sat quietly enjoying his second cup of coffee.

He glanced out the window and noticed Nancy heading toward the office. Burt's eyes met Maggie's and spoke to her saying, "Your indignant guest wants some attention!"

Maggie looked out the window and saw Nancy's amazing bouffant hairdo pass by. Nancy flung open the screen door and let it slam, interrupting Maggie's train of thought.

Maggie thought to herself, "Now what?"

"Louie you stole my bra! I want to be compensated for it!" exclaimed Nancy.

"I only seized control over a crisis situation!" Louie said.

Burt interceded and pleaded for calm from both parties. When Burt found out that Louie had mutilated a classic Playtex Long-Line bra, he hit the roof.

CHAPTER 10

PUZZLING BEHAVIOR
1963

A few days later, Maggie saw an oddly dressed woman walking across the parking lot. The woman had on a dress that was made out of scarves, loose fitting with bold colors. Maggie followed her. Maggie glanced in the window of her cottage and was dumbfounded when she noticed a blinking neon sign with a woman on it gazing into a crystal ball.

Soon afterward, Maggie started noticing cars coming and going at all hours of the day and night, but she had mixed emotions about making an issue out of this situation. With the Inn in disrepair and funds limited, she needed to be more tolerant of paying guests and stay determined to make up for lost revenue.

Over the next few weeks, Maggie tried to unintentionally on purpose run into Madame Zoshia and engage her in conversation but was never successful.

The woman was an expert at diversionary tactics, "I would love to stay and chat with you Maggie but I am headed out to the farmers market in East Jordan." "If you don't get there early, all the heirloom tomatoes are gone." Maggie took note later in the day that as she passed Zoshia's cottage, she could hear the voice of a woman with a thick European accent. "That is odd," she thought to herself.

When Maggie started seeing flyers in town for Tarot card readings, she knew she had to take action. Naturally there was speculation, most of it coming from Burt and the staff at the Inn who thought the gypsy just another bull shit artist, but soon discovered she had a very real and practical talent for locating missing jewelry.

That same day, Maggie observed her new guest surveying the property with a metal detector. The main thing Maggie seemed suspicious about was how a woman so well spoken and charming was able to win over so many of the local people in such a short period of time.

LET'S GET TO THE HEART OF THE MATTER

Maggie found herself at her kitchen table the next evening thinking, "Am I judging Miss Riddle harshly and does she really have a kind heart?"

Earlier in the day, Maggie accidently ran into her at the post office, and read the envelope she was mailing. It was addressed to Fay Merriweather in Buffalo, New York. She was out of breath when she told Maggie, "I send money every week to my sick, elderly aunt in Buffalo." With tears in her eyes, Zoshia recounted the story about her aunt Fay. As a child, her aunt was emphatic to her in ways her mother was not. She always provided a warm dinner and a shoulder to cry on.

What Zoshia really remembered more than anything else was the dress. Back in the summer of 1933, all the girls in her freshman class at Niagara High School talked incessantly about what they were going to wear the first day of school. She begged her mother to take her to Sattlers Department Store in downtown Buffalo to shop for a new outfit.

Promises were made but never kept. Aunt Fay took Zoshia with her on the bus to Sattlers and bought her a simple dress but as far as she was concerned it was the most beautiful dress in the world. And it was.

The glow in her face and sparkle of her eyes on that first day of school, made her stand out. She never forgot that day and never forgot her aunt Fay who made it happen.

CHAPTER 11

THE SO CALLED ASPISICIOUS ADVENTURES OF LOUIE MAY 1963

At one time, Louie had these fantasies that never came to fruition. He learned very quickly that if he did not want to be the laughing stock of East Jordan, he needed to go far away. In his attempts to realize his dreams-Elvis Impersonator, Comedian, Magician, Bouncer, Carnival Barker, and Stevedore, Tuesday mornings would frequently find Louie at the East Jordan Public Library scanning Michigan Sunday Newspapers for entertainment opportunities. Unfortunately, he had a fear of open places. Burt found him once, cowering in a lifeboat in Charlevoix.

Louie was always borrowing Burt's tools, and it drove him crazy, which led to many arguments. Louie had a couple years of maintenance experience from working at the East Jordan High School and according to his old supervisor, Ernest, "The job was at odds with his personality." He claimed he was a "People person" but in reality, he really liked to be left alone.

Louie's mother, Eleanor Larkin who owned the Chat and Chew Café, did the best she could raising Louie, considering his father, Gerald went off to the war in 1941. All of the fun that they shared, came to an abrupt end with World War II. His father died shortly after he returned in 1945. He had been all over in Europe, fighting against the Nazis, made it back home and then contracted pneumonia. Eleanor managed to keep the Café open with the capable help of Maggie's father, Sam, and Louie, as he got older.

As for Sam, he tried to act as a fatherly figure to Louie, but it was challenging. He hoped to do more to help Louie, but Sam had his own family responsibilities. When Louie was a teenager, Maggie remembered her father storming into the house through the back door one mid-summers day. Sam wouldn't talk about it, but Burt was willing to share the events that took place when Maggie inquired.

"I was fishing with your father on Lake Charlevoix, and we heard a mysterious cacophony of hoots and wails coming from a nearby boat. As we got closer, we had the privilege of discovering Louie in a boat that listed to one side with three, topless teenage girls in it. They were playing a game Louie called, 'rub-a-dub,'" said Burt. "Another demonstration of his low standards," Burt chimed in eagerly, but like Groucho Marx, secretly he came to the conclusion of, "A man's only as old as the woman he feels."

Louie knew all he needed was that one big break. His eyes lit up when he saw a notice for open mic night at Escanaba's Shimmy Sham Club. The drive to Escanaba was rough and took seven hours including a drive across the Mackinac Bridge. He showed up at the club only to discover that five minutes at the mic would cost him $5.00. He worried if he would make it home with the money he had in his pocket. The wait seemed endless. Then suddenly the MC announced, "Let's have a big round of applause for the comedy stylings of Louie Larkin from East Jordan."

Louie faltered onto the stage and the glare of the spotlights left him momentarily speechless. He was like a deer in the headlights. Once he got started and into his rhythm he felt he was doing well. That's when a half bottle of Schlitz whizzed by his head and crashed into the brick wall behind him. This unleashed a torrent of refuse directed at him and the stage. Louie ducked and took cover.

It was only when he was headed back home that he wondered whether he got his full five minutes at the Mic and whether he should return to get a partial refund. Other similar ventures into the entertainment industry did not go much better. However, Louie ever the obvious optimist, was not discouraged, "Maybe I am destined to work behind the scenes…as a writer, producer or an agent! I bet you that's where the real money is made."

"I need some business cards!"

CHRISTMAS TREE TRIMMERS
JUNE 1963

Burt and Bob glanced over to a couple of tables in the Chat and Chew where two groups of young men were sitting, waiting to be served. The Christmas tree trimmers descended on lunchtime in East Jordan during the summer months. They made their living by trimming Christmas trees over near Mancelona. They were quite a sight to see coming down the street, each one wearing a piece of stovepipe on one of their legs, and carrying a machete. One of the trimmers was overheard saying, "The Christmas tree business can be frustrating, but customers like the ones in Detroit, make it all worthwhile."

CHAPTER 12

WINSTON RENTS THE CABIN
JUNE 1963

Winston Worthington traveled the black tops of Antrim and Charlevoix counties, searching for accommodations.

"Where is it," he thought. "It has to be here…the down-on-its-heels motel. The Riviera, the Shangri-La, the Sanssouci, a tourist motel that had seen its better days." One of those places featured a neon sign, which sparkled and sizzled, its light flashing enticingly. He drove the speed limit, day dreaming so he almost missed the rambling old Inn but a glimpse through the pines required that further inspection was necessary.

He slowed the green, 1960 Dodge Van onto the roadside and back up some 100 yards in a cloud of dust. He drove down the long, winding driveway, a beautiful canopy of pine trees. He parked at the far end of the parking lot, the better to inspect the accommodations. The Whispering Pines Inn had settled into a state of ignorant bliss. The place cried for a fresh coat of paint and a new roof. That being said, the setting was spectacular. He saw 100-year-old White Pines, expansive grounds and an alluring view of the lake. He gasped with pleasure as tucked back into the pines he spied four white Tourist cabins, precisely the situation he had so desperately searched for.

Winston donned his tufted sport coat and cap, approached the door slowly, and tapped on the wooden screen lightly and soon a matronly, 85 year old lady opened the screen.

"Yes, can I help you?" Adeline asked.

"Yes mam, yes indeed. I be looking for some summer accommodations."

CHAPTER 13

ANTIQUE BOAT SHOW
JUNE 1963

Winston Worthington had a fixation with transportation—every day he sat outside near the harbor and stared at the old steam engine in East Jordan.

Winston enjoyed talking to the guests at the Inn about his memory of being shipped out on a tramp steamer after being in Istanbul. It was all fabricated. Some of the people from the Inn observed him trying to make headway with Johanna and repeating the same story again and again.

Louie had his own opinion of Winston and just that morning said to Burt, "I think he is another quintessential acid causality."

Winston felt humiliated when he thought about all of the times Johanna had ignored him. That was all about to change.

At around ten o'clock on a hazy Saturday morning, Winston, a slightly stocky, 40ish man with extra poundage around the waist, (he was more annoyed at the decline of his body than anyone else) talked a vacationer from Chicago with a beautiful, antique Chris-

Craft into letting him use his boat that night for a brief moonlight cruise around the north arm of Lake Charlevoix. After congratulating himself ("I got this") Winston took a spin over to Grandma Sumner's Souvenir shop in Petoskey and bought a black and white captains hat.

All he could think of for the rest of the day was the Chris-Craft boat, and more seriously, getting to know Johanna better. It would be a great night for catching celestial light across the great Lake Michigan. Winston wanted his own Chris-Craft girl[8] to adorn his life.

For many who lived on the shore of Lake Michigan, sailing was a favorite pastime. For those who had a deep and abiding fascination with leisure and race boats, the Chris-Craft boats and the girls whose lives were intertwined with them[9], stood out; they were rooted in the hearts and minds of all who work or play on the water.

The shark circled the tank and approached Johanna a couple hours later in the dining room at the Inn. Johanna was just finishing her coffee with dinner when Winston leaned in. Ready for action, Winston finally saw his chance to be with Johanna and get over his defeatist attitude.

"I understand the walnut chocolate fudge at Murray's in Charlevoix is quite the aphrodisiac," he said in a persuasive voice.

Johanna agreed to go to the Boyne City Antique Boat Show that evening with Winston.

---

8 "There's a wholesome and refreshing air about her. Hundreds of Chris-Craft girls have adorned the decks and bridges of the world's largest fleet of boats. Since the 1920's, they have helped to stir the imaginations of millions of sailors, both real and imaginary, through the pages of the brochures, catalogs and magazines where Chris-Craft products have been displayed.

9 Though she can range in age from 3 to 93, she is urgently alive, blushing with health, and has been a role model for five generations of youthful America."

As he maneuvered the magnificent mahogany boat named Winngagami, with teak and brass and with a yacht ensign flag blowing behind them in the wind, he felt like the master of his own destiny for the first time in his life.

He displayed a remarkable knowledge of antique boats, particularly the Chris-Craft Boat Company.

Wearing white Ray Ban glasses and a brown wide-brimmed hat, Johanna asked him,

"How are you so knowledgeable in this regard?"

Winston said, "It's in my blood!"

The authoritative text on wooden speed boats, the history of the Chris Craft Company and gold cup racing had been returned to the East Jordan library several days prior to this boat show. Johanna had been lured in.

They cruised slowly past vacationers on the beach, who were packing up their pink and white striped beach umbrella and Coleman cooler. Johanna felt a soft wind blow through her hair. The sun was retreating and she saw a fireworks display off in the distance, coming from Boyne City.

The next thing you know, they were gone for four hours.

When they returned they saw the distraught owner of the boat standing on the dock with binoculars inquiring,

"Where have you been?!"

Johanna's buttons were off kilter.

Winston had some red lipstick on his shirt and face.

Winston replied, "With all due respect sir, I saw another boat stalled in the middle of the lake so I had to offer a tow home. Little did I know that the owner docked his boat in East Jordan! It was a long tow down through the south arm of Lake Charlevoix!"

He complimented the owner on owning a masterpiece of a boat.

"Sir, I even managed to get the hard cushions back in place!" Winston exclaimed jokily.

Winston tried to make light of the situation but the owner was not amused.

Trying hard to impress Johanna, Winston kissed her hand and said, "Merci pour les bonnes moments."

He tied it up and hurried Johanna away from the scene of this latest escapade. They headed back to the Inn.

"What just happened there?" she asked.

"We commandeered a boat!" Winston said.

Winston liked to have a good time and he was not above borrowing something without permission. People always forgave him because that's just Winston and he meant no harm.

"It is not a burden I am going to carry," he told himself.

Johanna was not one to get herself attached to just one man. She was a bit of a free spirit and forgot about Winston pretty quickly. She saw a new fellow, Gus, on the horizon.

CHAPTER 14

NYSTROM BAR SCENE
JUNE 1963

Geology professor Johanna Nystrom dragged herself through the lobby of the Whispering Pines, dusty and sore. She carried a beige rucksack over one shoulder and a black and silver Minolta camera around her neck. The rucksack contained stones. She had spent the day traipsing around Charlevoix County examining and photographing geological formations, particularly drumlins, and collecting rock samples. She was now faced with the tiresome task of cataloguing her day's work and trying to make sense of what, if anything, she had accomplished. Miss Nystrom had forgotten how exhausting field work could be. All she wanted was a hot shower and a long nap.

A week ago, Johanna was clunking around in the Upper Peninsula doing research west of Marquette. She was fascinated with ancient granites, the iron formations and the copper bearing rocks. These are referred to collectively as Precambrian. Johanna studied the area for several weeks. She discovered, that nearly two billion years ago, this area was very likely as high the Alps. She speculated that this region may even have been as high as the present-day Himalaya Mountains, the tallest peaks in the world.

Johanna never married and considered herself plain. She took pride in her simple style.

As she passed by the double glass door entrance to the restaurant, she glanced into the mahogany paneled tavern. Afternoon sunlight cast inviting amber warmth over the establishment.

George, the steadfast barkeep, was alone, slicing limes and listening to NPR.

"Why not?" Johanna thought. "Just one."

"Hello George."

"Hello Miss Nystrom. What's your pleasure?"

"I'll have a Stroh's."

"Certainly."

George reached for a bottle of Stroh's from the cooler, poured it into a chilled beer schooner and presented it to his customer. He then walked down to the other end of the bar, giving Miss Nystrom some space. He idly picked up a beer glass and began polishing out the water spots. Miss Nystrom appraised herself in the opulent back bar mirror, ran her fingers through her long auburn hair, gave up and took a long sip of beer. She then looked up at George, and the barkeep, sensing by professional intuition that she desired some company, wandered back toward her.

"I trust you had a productive day?" he asked, nodding at her rucksack.

"Oh yes," she answered.

"In this beautiful country, every day is productive."

He waited. It was up to her to decide what she wanted him to know about her day, about her stay at the inn, about herself.

"Okay," she thought. "I'm a geology professor," she volunteered.

"I teach at the University up at Sault Sainte Marie. I'm on sabbatical. Copper and iron ore mines got too tedious for me. I decided to explore the northern Southern peninsula—drumlins, giant granite boulders, Petoskey stones and all that....and sunlight, the glorious sunlight."

She paused. She had already revealed enough.

"Geology. Who would have guessed?" George answered.

"Never pictured you as one of those spelunkers. Geology," George repeated.

He paused. "I trust your stay has been pleasant?" he eventually inquired.

This seemingly innocuous question dripped with innuendo, if not in George's mind, then at least in Johanna's.

For Miss Nystrom had become a regular attendee at Mr. Gus Campbell's nightly bacchanals and, in recent weeks, her nightly visits had stretched into sunrise.

"My fling... (No! It isn't a fling. Oh hell! I don't know what it is.)...must be common knowledge by now. Yes, and who else knows about her extracurricular activities?" she pondered.

"Yes. My stay has been most pleasant," she replied.

"Geology," he said again, incredulously.

"Yes. Geology," she answered.

She hesitated, decided to take the plunge and continued:

"Look. I know that Gus Campbell is full of the blarney. It's pure, unadulterated bullshit. Nonsense. Gibberish. But there's just enough truth and knowledge to keep me coming back for more. I mean c'mon. The Colossus of Rhodes on a leeward tack!"

George nodded in understanding.

"Aah. The Colossus of Rhodes, always a treacherous passage even in the calmest of seas," George observed.

Miss Nystrom burst out laughing and George joined in. Her laughter was irresistible. She held up her glass in toast and drained her beer. George nodded and smiled.

"If I ever do sail under Mr. Rhodes, I do hope he's colossus," she observed as she headed out the door.

GUEST LECTURE
EARLY JUNE 1963

But perhaps Gus Campbell's most memorable escapade was not a campfire bacchanal, a sexual conquest or another outrageous excursion gone awry. For in fact, by happenstance, Mr. Campbell was invited to present a guest lecture to the History class at the local high school. Mr. Smith, the East Jordan High School history, geography and liberal arts teacher (Brown, '59) first met Mr. Campbell at downtown East Jordan's Locomotive Park.

Mr. Smith oftentimes took his sack lunch to the park, weather permitting, to escape the bedlam of the high school. Mr. Campbell frequently visited the park simply to enjoy the view of the Jordan River headwaters as they emptied into Lake Charlevoix and, more particularly, to marvel at the power and the grace of the East Jordan & Southern No. 6 Locomotive, (a 2-6-0 built by ALCO in 1909), enshrined there. He and Winston had something in common.

On this particular day, Mr. Smith noticed Mr. Campbell eyeing his peach and offered it to him. Mr. Campbell declined, explaining that peaches were out of season and that he preferred only Georgia peaches. The teacher, always on the lookout for a receptive audience, began to launch into a soliloquy on the Detroit Tigers' great outfielder, Ty Cobb, nicknamed the Georgia Peach. Campbell politely interrupted, explaining that he was referring to peaches not from the state of Georgia, USA but from the republic of Georgia in the Soviet Union. Mr. Smith was intrigued.

From that day forward, world traveler and armchair traveler would meet at the park Tuesdays and Thursdays, eat lunch and Smith would sit back and listen to tales of adventure from the far reaches' of the world.

Mr. Smith considered himself a progressive teacher. He attempted to engage his students with visual aids, movies, field trips and unique homework assignments. A guest lecture from a world traveler would be just the right ticket as classes wound down toward summer. And so it came to pass that Mr. Gus Campbell found himself standing in front of 30 indifferent high school students to present his guest lecture "Wonders of the Mediterranean."

The lecture predictably began at the rock of Gibraltar and proceeded north through Spain, with emphasis upon its rich artistic heritage from Goya to Salvadore Dali. Things moved splendidly along, Mr. Campbell speaking clearly and coherently and the students politely ignoring him. Smith quietly excused himself from the classroom and hastened to the teacher's lounge for a break.

The lecture proceeded around the Mediterranean coast toward the Cote d'Azur, but first, Campbell observed, "A lecture on the Mediterranean would not be complete without a discussion of its commercial, industrial, and transportation Centre, Marseille."

"I could speak for hours about the importance of Marseille but one attraction stands out above all the rest…the docks." Mr. Campbell's voice rose steadily as he warmed to his subject.

"And on the docks one attraction must be singled out as most noteworthy…the HARLOTS."

With these words, the class, a somnolent beast, wakened and stretched.

"What's a harlot?" a student whispered to a classmate.

"What's a harlot?" the lecturer repeated. "Yes, my good boy, a most incisive question."

And thus, Campbell seamlessly segued into the real purpose of his high school lecture—a public service pronouncement on the dangers of venereal disease.

1963—the pill had been approved by the FDA and was gaining popularity.

"Louie, Louie" was #2 on the pop charts and "The Watusi" and "Heatwave" were popular hits. Teens did not dance, they shook and gyrated. With this alarming tumescence of teenage lust, who would take a stand for virtue and chastity? At EJHS that man was Gus Campbell.

"A harlot, a cornucopia of earthly delights, and a garden of sexual bliss, a phantasmagorical…" he really had them now… "Pleasure palace."

"A harlot is also…" he leaned forward, his voice barely a whisper… "Is also a pestilent, pustulent, purulent purveyor of diabolical disease, commonly known as—THE CLAP!"

"Who here has seen a full blown, raging case of the clap?" A student in the back finally engaged in a subject he could relate to, thrust his arm in the air and then quickly pulled it down. Another young man shot a furtive, piercing look at a pretty female across the room. She buried her head in her hand, pretending to take notes.

"The CLAP, my young friends with the newly developed bodies and the raging hormones, is a potpourri of syphilis, gonorrhea and chlamydia…" The lecture labored on, guys squeezing their testicles between their thighs and girls folding their arms over their chests. It was at the propitious moment that Campbell utilized the blackboard to illustrate male and female anatomy, infested and disease free, that the assistant principal, Mr. Rutgers, making his rounds, saw a stranger drawing obscene stick figures in front of a class of juniors and put a screeching halt to the proceedings.

CHAPTER 15

IRV GOES MISSING
JUNE 1963

A prominent feature of the Whispering Pines stately lobby was the oil portrait of its founder, Irving Feldman. It was commissioned in 1942, and Mr. Feldman said he was, "Inspired to have his portrait painted" because of Henry Wallace, Vice President of the United States at that time, who had proclaimed the dawning of the "Century of the Common Man."

Mr. Feldman hung above the fireplace, gazing down judgmentally upon the resort's guests. The portrait depicted Mr. Feldman in profile, his right hand on chin, his piercing eyes surveying his domain. Evinrude, his beloved Basset Hound, lay languorously across his lap. Mr. Feldman appears to be wrestling with the meaning of life and Evinrude appears bored to tears.

The most compelling aspect of the portrait is Irving Feldman's piercing stare. He glares down upon his resort clientele with self-righteous indignation. One can only conclude that with Innkeeper Irving Feldman still at the helm things would have operated differently.

In early June, Inn proprietor Maggie realized that it had been far too long since she had conducted an inspection tour of the Inn property. As housekeeping manager, as food, beverage and entertainment manager and as office manager she made regular inspections of her territory. As Inn proprietor, she feared what she would find and delayed the onerous task for as long as possible. She could not procrastinate any longer.

Innkeeper Sanders had no sooner commenced her inspection tour when she noticed that Irving Feldman had flew the coop.

There, above the fireplace where the portrait of Mr. Feldman once hung was a blank rectangle of virgin pine. Maggie stood mystified. "Who in hell would want to steal that?" she mused.

Maggie cast her eyes about the lobby and noticed, for the first time, that other pictures were missing. A 19th century tintype photo of William F. Empey, East Jordan's founder, had disappeared. An "American Gothic" style portrait of the first couple to homestead on the present site of Whispering Pines was also missing. Inquiries to staff were to no avail. The mystery remained unsolved.

A couple of days later, on business errands in East Jordan, Maggie walked past the Regrettable & Forgettable Resale Shoppe and halted in her tracks. There, prominently displayed in the resale Shoppe window, hung the oil portrait of Whispering Pines founder Irving Feldman.

Maggie rushed inside and studied the likeness in closer detail.

A clerk quickly approached her and said, "Quite a formidable portrait, wouldn't you say?"

"Yes," Maggie answered. "May I inquire? How did you manage to acquire this interesting piece?"

"We just got a new consignment in. Some very unique items of local interest. A reclusive collector decided it was time to liquidate."

"I'd love to see them."

As the clerk escorted Maggie around the store, Maggie identified a number of paintings, old photographs, and bric-a-brac, which she recognized. The clerk noticed her dismay.

"I feel a Deja vu. Like these antiques are speaking to me," Maggie explained. "Yeah, like telling me to call the sheriff," Maggie thought to herself. "This collector. Is she a slender, elegantly dressed middle-aged woman with an English accent?" Maggie asked evasively.

The clerk moved closer and lowered her voice to a whisper.

"No. Actually I think she's Eastern European, very exotic, an older woman with a flair for the flamboyant. But very personable. Once you meet her, you feel like you've been friends forever."

"Wears a babushka, lots of jewelry. The scent of White Shoulders. Plus size, sandals, rolled hose?" Maggie inquired.

"That's her all right," the clerk responded.

Maggie had heard enough. She raced out of the store and sped down M-66, to the Inn. She pulled up in front of Zoshia's guest cabin in a cloud of dust. The damnable neon fortune teller's crystal ball was blinking. Zoshia was in. Maggie pounded on the door.

A red-checkered curtain fluttered slightly and then Zoshia opened the door. "What a pleasant surprise. Please come in." Zoshia's politeness was off putting.

"I've come from the Regrettable & Forgettable Resale Shoppe. What the hell is going on?" said Maggie.

"Ah. Now I understand. Let me explain." Zoshia guided Maggie across the Inn parking lot and into the lobby. There, on the wall above the fireplace, hung a large oil painting depicting the Whispering Pines in its Roaring Twenties heyday.

"It's a Williams, an early work, highly collectable. She's an East Jordan native. Her Hyannis Port seascapes go for tens of thousands of dollars. "Reefing the Jib" just sold at Sotheby's for $17,000. I discovered Whispering Pines at the resale. I made a deal."

CHAPTER 16

ZOSHIA'S CONFIDENCE GAME

During the annual spring barbecue held in the park in East Jordan, lots of green tents were set up. East Jordan Chamber of Commerce promoted the event in an effort to entice the people living in the community to spend their time and money at it. It was a way to encourage hospitality and worked to build friendships within the local community.

At twelve o'clock that afternoon, Zoshia had a plan. Every minute counted. She surveyed the park, found an empty tent, rushed to set up her card table, threw a yellow tablecloth over it and before she knew it she had a long line of people waiting to receive their tarot card reading.

When things started to slow down, she whipped around in the chair and decided to switch to Three-Card-Monty to make more money.

Zoshia didn't want to wake up from her dream world. Here in front of her, was the enthusiastic crowd who couldn't lose their money fast enough. "I just don't have the heart to turn them away," she thought.

As the afternoon waned, the crowd gradually dispersed. Zoshia's mind wandered. "How the hell did I ever get here?" she asked herself. It seemed to her that just moments ago she was a gay, carefree coed dreaming of a summer in France.

As long as she could remember, she imagined herself living in a Parisian loft, painting everyday street scenes along the Left Bank, visiting the Boulangerie, the Fromageri and sipping café au lait. She would become entranced by a local coureur de jupons, who would eventually break her heart.

Her daydream of what might have been was rudely interrupted when she saw one of her marks heading her way, accompanied by two of East Jordan's finest. She hurriedly picked up shop, hoping to slip out the back way. She found her exit blocked by a third police officer. "The jig's up, sister," she said to herself.

She decided to face the situation head on. "May I read your fortune, Officer Arnold?" she inquired, quickly glancing at his name tag. "Perhaps there's a woman in your future. And, of course, there is a discount for our men in blue," she offered. She could tell immediately by Officer Arnold's brush cut, his scuffed shoes and his Banquet chicken pot pie paunch that he was a confirmed bachelor.

Officer Arnold's cheeks turned red. He stammered. He was about to take Madame Zoshia up on her offer.

His partner, Officer Reid, stepped in. "Mam, we have a complaint that you are operating a gambling enterprise here on city property. You will need to come with us." She knew the drill. She turned around, placed her hands behind her back and remained still as the police officer cuffed her and led her to the squad car.

Necessitas non habet legem ("Necessity has no law")

All of the fun and laughter with the locals came to a sudden halt. Only one day after she came home from jail, the postman handed her an envelope with the summons in it. She was ordered to appear in The 90th District Court for the County of Charlevoix the following day on June 10, 1963 at 9:00 A. M.

Zoshia made a beeline to the Chat and Chew that afternoon and directed her supporters to "show up at court tomorrow morning."

She never assumed that they would, but by the next morning, as people showed up on motorcycles, bicycles, and hauling their coach trailer behind their automobiles, she greeted them with hugs and kisses. Zoshia, unbeknownst to council, also brought several carloads of enthusiastic supporters with her. This motley crew of East Jordan's finest malingers supplied a boisterous cheering section for the wrongly accused victim.

As Miss Riddle was ushered into the courtroom by her attorney, she learned she was not the first case on the docket.

The Bailiff signaled the courtroom, "All rise. The 90th District Court for the County of Charlevoix is now in session. The Honorable Judge Edgar Bartlett presiding. Please be seated."

Judge Bartlett briskly entered the courtroom from his chambers, settled himself on the bench, cleared his throat and adjusted his microphone.

"Good morning, ladies and gentlemen," Judge Bartlett announced.

He then surveyed the gallery and was amazed to see that the oak benches were full and a number of people stood along the sides and back of the courtroom. Reporters from the East Jordan Town Crier and Traverse City Record Beagle sat in the front row, notebooks in hand, pencils posed.

Judge Bartlett moved the microphone, and whispered instructions to the Court Clerk.

She handed him a small stack of files. Typically, criminal cases were called first. The Court then proceeded to handle a typical assortment of criminal misdemeanors – speeding, DWI misdemeanor, Larceny, fishing without a license and possession of trout beyond legal size limit. Disposition of these cases made only a small dent in the courtroom crowd.

The crowd was agitated. One observer waved a "Free Zoshia" sign, which the Bailiff promptly confiscated and propped in a back corner of the courtroom.

The Court Clerk handed Judge Bartlett the People vs. Miss Riddle file, believing a prompt resolution of the matter would clear the courtroom.

"Please stand. Raise your right hand. Do you promise that the testimony you shall give in the case before this court shall be the truth, the whole truth, and nothing but the truth, so help you God?" said the Clerk.

"I do," Zoshia replied.

She was sworn in and sat down in the witness box.

"Please state your name and address for the record," said the prosecuting attorney.

"My name is Zoshia Riddle. Your honor before we go any further, I would like to voir dire the witness."

The Judge replied, "Madam, you are the witness."

"Precisely my point," she retorts. The Judge shook his head in confusion and glanced at his watch.

"Proceed," he said.

"Please state your address for the record," the prosecuting attorney repeated.

"My permanent address, my mailing address or my residential

address?" she inquires.

"Your legal address," the District Attorney responded emphatically.

Playing it straight, "What's a legal address?" Zoshia asked the Judge.

Judge Bartlett started to respond but the peanut gallery started a face off.

"Their trying to confuse her," proclaimed a loud voice from the back of the courtroom. "It's a railroad job."

"The fix is in." "I know she's a shyster, but she's an honest shyster," said one of her supporters to no one in particular. His neighbors nodded in agreement.

Another observer declared, "This is a travesty of justice!" drowning out the Judges' voice.

"Order. Order in this court!" Judge Bartlett commanded, banging his gavel. Suddenly a blue flip-flop sailed past the Judge's head into a large framed, black and white photograph of President Eisenhower.

A wave of laughter swept through the courtroom.

The Judge pushed a panic button underneath his bench and additional Deputy Sheriffs quickly appeared at the back of his courtroom.

Meanwhile, there were people protesting out in front of the courthouse.

Madam Riddle's onlookers, noticing the added security, calmed themselves down.

"If I have any further disturbances in my court room I will clear the court," declared the Judge.

"Bailiff, look for a person with only one flip-flop."

A few minutes later, with order restored, the Judge looked at the large black clock with roman numerals and announced, "Well, we have made quite a bit of progress this morning, and I see that now would be a good time to break for lunch.

Court will recess and be back in session at 1:30 P.M."

The onlookers checked their watches and it was twelve o'clock. As the Assistant District Attorney picked up his case file, the Judge gave him a meaningful glare which even a neophyte attorney understood to mean that he better get a plea from this defendant or life could get miserable.

"All rise," the Bailiff announced.

The Judge left the bench thinking, "Yale Law, for this group of patsies? To think those ne'er-do-wells out there are my constituents. I depend on their vote for my livelihood."

The court reassembled and at 1:35 P.M. the plea deal was guilty of perpetuating a public nuisance. Sentence was time served and 60 hours of community service.

At that moment, the Judge said, "I urge you to put your math skills to better use Miss Riddle."

SUMMER SCHOOL

The very next day, Zoshia met with the High School Head Counselor and made arrangements to tutor students struggling with math. Her tutoring sessions were closely monitored at first by the head of the math department. All seemed to be going well. The math department was pleased with her effort.

Summer school started and she was more or less left to her own devices. All of the teachers in the math department were on their summer vacation now. She was instructed to reaffirm the math lessons taught during the school year and bolster the students' confidence. They soon became bored with the same old math lessons and she had to agree with them.

The hot sun poured through the paned glass windows with oak

trim molding in the old classroom the following morning. The smell of white pine trees filled the air.

Zoshia stood at the doorway, feeling melancholy, with her arms folded. She watched the teenagers as they awkwardly laughed and entertained each other all the way down the hall.

Five pupils walked slowly into the blistering heat and she wondered what she could possible teach them that day. Nevertheless, it dawned on her that five or six was an ideal number for a poker game. The students found it pleasurable and for all of them it became a favorite summer day that would remain a fond memory for the rest of their lives. Little did they know that their belief and confidence in her had toppled all of her past transgressions, and was leading her to want to become a better person.

Back at her cottage that night, Zoshia turned on her radio. "Gypsy Woman," sung by The Impressions was playing. She leaned back in a green, upholstered arm chair, and looked up at the ceiling. She thought about the events of the past couple of months at the Inn and those young people she tutored today.

"Was she living up to her promise to Aunt Fay to always do the right thing?" she wondered.

"Don't be a fool anymore," she thought in a reflective mood.

She smiled to herself, and decided she needed to find a new sense of purpose.

Feeling a need to unburden herself, she wrote a letter of apology worthy of a response from "Dear Abby," addressed it to Maggie, and left it on top of the gray Formica kitchen table next to the keys to the cottage. Zoshia wrote that deep down inside she didn't intentionally mean to harm anyone.

She packed up her crystal ball, neon sign and other personal belongings. It was time to go.

CHAPTER 17

CHEF SAVES SALLY

Chef Claude began noting Sally's mood swings in early June, 1963. One night she would be energetic, invested, top of the world; the next morose, stay away, the weight of the world on her shoulders. Chef initially chalked it up to normal growing pains but an incident he witnessed one evening changed his mind. It was a slow weeknight and the restaurant staff knocked off early.

Sally walked out to the parking lot with a few other girls, laughing, making plans on where to go. The night was still young. It was then Sally noticed a skinny, grubby looking guy in his early twenties leaning against a 1957 Brown Chevy Bel Air.

"Johnnie, what are you doing here?" she asked. She approached him.

Their conversation grew more animated and quickly turned into a heated argument. Sally started to walk away. The kid grabbed her arm, twisted her around and pushed her to his car. One girl started to go after her but another told her not to get involved.

"It's all right. Maybe another night," Sally called back as she got in the car.

The kid spun his tires on the gravel and sped off. Sally came to work the next night with a bruise on her left arm.

From that day forward, Chef monitored Sally's work departures. On nights when Johnnie picked her up, she slid into the car without a word. If he had to wait, he'd be pissed. Chef tried to casually inquire about Sally's situation.

"That's Johnnie. He's bad news," one dishwasher volunteered.

"A girl's gotta do what a girl's gotta do," another shrugged.

"Not one of my girls," Chef thought.

Chef Claude had left a daughter at home in Lyon, France. His culinary travels included prestigious stints in Alsace, Nice, Singapore and St. Bart's. His family history included several love affairs, a divorce, a drinking problem and a distant daughter. For some inexplicable reason, Sally of East Jordan, Michigan had touched a nerve.

"Why didn't I do something? Why didn't I intervene?" Chef asked himself.

"It happened so fast by the time it was happening it was over," he realized.

Shortly after, Chef Claude created a scheduling mix-up so that he could offer Sally a ride home.

"I need to go to town to pick up some ingredients," he explained. "It's no problem."

Sally rode along as Chef drove through East Jordan and continued south. A few miles out of town Sally directed Chef to pull off the road by a long gravel driveway. Set far back off the road was a neat ranch home, adjacent to a large pole barn.

"Well, here we are. Home sweet home," Sally announced, not too convincingly. She began walking up the driveway, waving, waiting for Chef to pull away.

Chef was more convinced than ever that something was not

right. He drove off, searching for the next crossroad. He found a farmer's two-track, swung around, and headed back in the direction he had come. He pulled off to the side of the road and waited five minutes.

He didn't want Sally to catch him spying on her. When he backtracked past the ranch house, Sally was nowhere to be found. No trace of her anywhere on the road.

"Could she actually live there?" Chef seriously doubted it.

It was on his third attempt that he spotted her in the distance, cutting down a path between a cornfield and a fencerow. Next time, he swung around the mile square section and watched her reappear at the north side of the field. From the vantage point of a farm lane, Chef Claude watched as Sally walked up to a dilapidated farmhouse. The home had two stories, constructed of large white brick. Half the roof was covered by a large black tarp. The front yard was littered with a John Deere riding lawn mower, a junker car, and a rusted car motor up on cinder blocks and several bikes in various stages of disrepair. By the front porch an old red wagon held several pots of flowers…the only ray of sunshine in a sea of destitution.

Chef crept from his car to the edge of the cornfield. As Sally neared the front steps, Chef noticed three guys sitting on the porch, passing a joint.

"Where you been, bitch?" a scrawny long-haired kid called out. He threw an empty beer can at her. The other two laughed.

"I'm hungry," he declared.

Chef had seen enough. He drove back to the Inn, his hand squeezing the wheel in spasms of anger, dismay and frustration. By eleven o'clock that night he had formulated a plan.

The next morning, Chef met with Maggie to apprise her of the situation, received her full support, got a haircut at Bob's, and stopped by the Overbeck farm to speak to Hans, the big, strong

German who supplied his beef. That night, Chef told Sally, "I'm going to knock off early. I gotta go to town. I'll drop you off at home."

Sally shrugged and followed him out the door.

As Chef drove out of the parking lot, a 1958, green Chrysler New Yorker swung in behind him. Bob drove. Hans rode shotgun.

"What the hell! I moved out of Detroit to get away from all this nonsense and now I'm wheelman in a kidnapping!" Bob exclaimed.

"And I'm the muscle," Hans declared.

"I just don't want no trouble," Bob said.

"Have you seen this kid Johnnie? I promise you there will be no trouble," Hans replied.

Chef Claude skipped the usual charade and drove directly to Sally's house. He pulled into the driveway and drove right up to the house. The New Yorker stopped right behind.

"Will somebody tell me what's going on?" Sally demanded.

"Go get your stuff. You're not staying here a night longer. I don't want any arguments," Chef commanded.

He followed her into the house and stood at the bottom of the stairs. Bob and Hans stood in the hallway, arms crossed, trying to look tough. Johnnie laid on the sofa, staring at the TV, half gone. A roommate came out of the kitchen and surveyed the situation. Sally was rushing up and down the stairs with garbage bags in her hand.

"Hey Johnnie, these old guys are movin' Sally out," he said.

Johnnie straightened up momentarily, and checked things out.

"Screw Sally. Those old guys can go to hell," he declared and went back to his TV.

Sally hurried out to Chef Claude's car and the two vehicles drove off. The New Yorker stopped in town. Chef and Sally rode in silence.

Finally, Sally asked, "Where am I going to stay now?"

"You're going to stay with me," he answered. He felt her stiffen.

"No funny…" Sally didn't finish. Claude had turned toward her and glared.

They reached the Inn, parked and carried her belongings up the gravel path toward Chef Claude's tourist cabin.

"I'll sleep on the couch," she declared.

"No, you won't sleep on the couch." She stopped, moved away.

"You'll sleep in your bed, in your own bedroom," Chef told her.

He kept walking, past his old cabin, to a newly refurbished two-bedroom cottage further back in the pines.

"My own bed?!" she said, half question, half incredulous statement.

"I never had my own bed." Tears welled up in her eyes. They walked a little farther.

"No late nights. No mischief," he declared. She smiled with tears in her eyes.

"People will talk," she said.

"People always talk," he replied.

"Then there's no problem?" she asked.

"Do you have a problem? I don't have a problem," Chef answered.

"OK Pops."

He went to wrap his burly arm around her shoulder but hesitated. She leaned against his side and looked up at him, her eyes full of gratitude.

"Pops," he thought. "Pops. Yeah, I like it. Not Dad, not Father, but 'Pops,' a nickname, casual but showing respect. 'Pops.'"

THE ZOO
1963

The flowers appear on the earth, the time of singing has come, and the voice of the turtledove is heard in our land. - Song of Solomon 2:12

Summer was in full force when some of the residents at the Inn decided to adopt a reptile at the local zoo in Petoskey. It was a large snapping turtle and his name was Edwin.

Pretty soon everyone started getting in arguments about the turtles diet, leisure time, living space and exercise. Some even started writing to relatives in other cities as to the care and rearing of snapping turtles.

The zookeeper reported one day to Maggie that the turtle had gone missing.

A search ensued.

Early the next day, a knock came to Maggie's office door. Miss Kelly, a counselor at the high school and tutor during the summer, who finished her work day at the Sperry Hotel, swore that the turtle sat on the bar stool next to her for at least two hours.

When asked to describe what she remembered of that night she said, "All I remember are the clammy hands!"

There were rumors that the turtle descended into the sewers. Needless to say, the "Adopt a Pet" program was disbanded at the Inn.

CHAPTER 18

BEEHIVE INCIDENT

On Saturday morning, June 21, 1963, Maggie began receiving complaints about bees pestering guests on the patio. She at first attributed the problem to food debris left in trash receptacles about the property and gave specific directions to empty these trash bins twice per day. She considered the problem solved. Complaints persisted and an employee was stung. A search for the culprit's nest ensued and a giant beehive was discovered under an eave at the far south end of the Inn.

Maggie cleverly avoided the expense of an exterminator. She assembled her own crack team of exterminators in-house and gave them a very specific tutorial on the elimination of bees nests, gleaned from observing her own father's battles with bee problems in her youth.

"Do not try to burn them out. Do not try to use a bug bomb. Just wait until dark when the hive is quiet, rip the nest off the eave into a garbage bag and drown the nasty little varmints," she told them.

And so, the battle plan was in place. That very night she watched her bee hit squad assemble in the south side parking lot. Burt held a long stepladder and Louie carried a bucket with a box of garbage bags and several cans of bug spray. "Problem. Solution," Maggie glibly thought. The scheme initially proceeded according to schedule. The two employees patiently waited until dusk, periodically monitoring the beehive for decreased bee activity.

Finally, Burt set up the stepladder under the hive, climbed up and pulled a heavy black garbage bag from out of his black belt loop. He opened the garbage bag and, after a few practice passes, reached up and in one swift motion ripped the bees' nest off the eave and into the trash bag. He then deftly closed the bag with a few quick twists and passed it off to Louie, who was holding the ladder. "So far, so good," Maggie thought. "Well, this changes things, doesn't it?" said Maggie.

Lake Charlevoix has 56 miles of shoreline and a surface area of 17,200 acres. It is the third largest lake in Michigan. The lake is shaped like a horizontal Y with north and south arms joining a main branch, which runs through Round Lake, i.e. Charlevoix Harbor, and the Pine River channel into Lake Michigan. The maximum depth of Lake Charlevoix is 122 feet. In the south arm, by East Jordan the maximum depth is 58 feet. During the last several centuries Lake Charlevoix has witnessed a number of notable shipwrecks including the Mullen, the Avery, the Onekama, the Pottawatomie and the Keuka. The point being, Lake Charlevoix is large enough and deep enough to drown a hive of bees.

Maggie watched as Louie ran away from the shed holding the bees' nest at arm's length. Burt followed close behind. Maggie expected the two intrepid exterminators to proceed around the far corner of the Inn, skirt the edge of the Inn's expansive lakefront lawn and walk the bag of bees into the lake to meet their watery demise. Instead, the two scurried directly toward the Inn's front door. "No. No way. Stop, stop," Maggie shouted to herself.

She stood frozen in disbelief as she watched Burt open the

kitchen back entrance and hurry inside. "No way can this end well," Maggie thought. And indeed, it didn't.

Louie carried the garbage bag full of buzzing, angry bees into the inn, across the kitchen, and past a startled wait staff into the professional sized restaurant sink. The plan almost succeeded. Louie hastily dumped the garbage bag into the sink, loosened his grip, fitted the opening of the bag of bees under the faucet and turned on the spigot. A blast of scalding hot water made him release his grip. He valiantly tried to recover but it was too late. The garbage bag opened wide and a swarm of very angry hostages, bent on revenge, rose up and stormed through the kitchen. The sound was deafening.

In the dining room, dinner service was winding down. Some customers lingered over coffee and after dinner drinks. Others waited for their checks. The wait staff seemed to have disappeared on smoke breaks. Not for long. Dumbfounded diners watched the double doors into the kitchen burst open and belch out a bevy of kitchen staff, from waiters to line cooks to dishwashers, followed by a swarm of pissed off bees prepared to die in defense of their queen.

Arms flailed, voices screamed, arms swatted. In the middle of the bedlam, one particularly immobilized employee shouted out "Bees! Run!" Restaurant patrons did just that, upturning chairs, knocking over wine glasses, grabbing up tips. A mass exodus ensued. The staff struggled fanatically to get through the dining room, out the screen doors onto the patio followed by the customers and a swarm of organized bees.

A few of the kitchen staff remained, fighting the good fight, but the battle was hopeless. Maggie poked her head out of the office and quickly determined that the restaurant, kitchen, and lobby were infested with bees. In a stroke of executive inspiration, she realized there was nothing she could do that hadn't already been done and that her presence was not required.

"Time to take wine inventory," she thought.

Maggie carefully walked down the back stairs into the basement and entered the wine cellar. Already there, sitting on three cases of wine and sipping a fine vintage Burgundy, was Chef Claude. Chef offered Maggie a glass. She momentarily hesitated, then accepted the glass, took a sip and let the rich bouquet of the wine envelop her mouth. Above them was heard the ominous buzz of bees, sporadically interrupted by crashes and screams. Maggie and Chef raised their glasses in toast. "Tchin. Tchin," said Chef. "Any port in a storm," Maggie answered.

CHAPTER 19

GIVE ME A DAY WHEN TIME STANDS STILL 1963

On the following Saturday morning, the same day that Maggie finished hiring teenagers to work as waiters for her summer staff, Burt overheard two guests from Bloomfield Hills talking about heading over to Beaver Island for the day.

"You better wait a couple days just to be safe and avoid the nor'easter," Burt said. The couple did not listen.

Robert and Cheryl O'Connor returned to the Inn for their 10-year wedding anniversary. They had spent their honeymoon there back in 1953. They had many fond memories of backwoods and backseats.

They decided to take the Beaver Islander ferryboat from Charlevoix to Beaver Island on a cloudy, windy Saturday morning. The weather forecast reflected the sober mood that would all too soon be shared by the tourists on the boat.

Cheryl was striking with her dark brown hair, white sandals, and a sleeveless red and white gingham dress. Robert's skin was tan, and he had blond hair and blue eyes. He could have been one of the Beach Boys. He wore white slacks, a blue polo shirt and white deck shoes. He smelled good too. Like English Leather.

Cheryl and Robert weathered the choppy waters, and high winds and were pleasantly surprised when a local guy handed them keys to his old 53' Jeep, as they exited the ferry. An old, red tugboat was tied up near the dock. Tied up near another dock, were two beautiful schooners, one red and the other navy blue, with their sails rolled up.

At around eleven o'clock, the weather had changed for the better. Gazing out at the water, they saw masts rise from the deck of a large sailboat as it made its way toward Charlevoix. Seagulls were suspended in mid-air as they flew against the wind.

This was their opportunity to explore the historical aspect of the island, which meant everything to them, being history professors. Before getting on their way, the couple made one stop at the Shamrock Bar to crack open a cold one and grab a sandwich. Outside, six bicycles were parked along the black railing leading up the steps into the bar. A couple of local guys were over in a corner, debating who caught the most trout, bass and perch that week.

Joe, the owner of the bar, and being cheap, was in the middle of dismantling a worthless electrical appliance to see how it worked when the couple walked in. It dawned on him at that moment, that the tourists probably didn't know the exciting history about Beaver Island and its early settlers.

"What's your poison?" Joe asked.

"We'll have two Harp Lagers please," Robert declared.

"Yes, you may have noticed that being on the Island is like going back in time to a simpler era. The Island has an extensive history with Irish roots and dramatic power struggles within the Mormon Church," Joe began.

Wide-eyed, Robert and Cheryl both nodded, and said, "Tell us more." Joe could summon attention when he wanted to.

"Many Irish men and women lived on Beaver Island long before the ill-fated Kingdom of James Jesse Strang was established. There were two settlements back in 1847, around the time Strang arrived to make his preliminary survey. According to census records from 1850, the island had a population of about 483 people, 74% of whom were Mormons," he told them.

The waitress behind the counter wiped the remainder of a chocolate milkshake off her face, stopped what she was doing, sat on a stool holding her face with both hands and listened intently.

She wore a pink uniform with a black apron, black trim and headband that held her beautiful red hair off her freckled-face. Aideen Sullivan was working just for the summer, saving all of her money for tuition to attend Michigan State University in the fall. Learning more about her Irish descendants, however remote, was intriguing.

Joe looked at Robert and Cheryl and said, "Before I continue, I think you are gonna need another drink," and on that note poured them two more beers.

"Was James Jesse Strang a gifted con man, who lived on the fringes of American society? That is what many who have explored the history of the Mormon kingdom established on Beaver Island in the 1850's believe. However, when you delve deeper, there is more to this story than meets the eye. He was a contradiction in many ways. He wrote a letter to Joseph Smith stating he was Smith's successor. The next thing he did was charge Brigham Young with polygamy, excommunicated him and then became a polygamist himself. During his time as a self-proclaimed King of Beaver Island, Strang declared a strict dress code on the Island and issued horsewhipping to anyone who wore finery. Strang, himself had no problem sporting a crimson robe and a jeweled crown. He took over government lands and gave them to his followers disguised as inheritances from God. Originally, he was opposed to polygamy, but once settled on the Island, he had five wives and fourteen children. None of this sat well with the majority of the islanders.

On June 16, 1856, while walking down the dock to the USS Michigan, a United States Naval vessel docked in the harbor, Strang was shot in the back by two local men who had been flogged by Strang in recent days.

Even though Strang had some issues cloaked in disguise, was it necessary to murder him? You be the judge," Joe stated.

Eager to learn more, the couple hurried off in their jeep, and drove deep into the woods. Dirt roads that skirted miles of pure white, sandy shoreline and showed off canopied towering emerald trees spoke to them. Locals waved as the couple drove past. Along the way, they discovered an old abandoned canoe and paddled out on a small lake a couple miles from the shoreline. They saw splashes of color from the abundant wildflowers growing in the woods. Blue heron, owls, beaver and loons were spotted and a magnificent American Bald Eagle flew overhead. Robert and Cheryl were enchanted by Beaver Island's rustic charm.

After a long day of driving up and down back roads, exploring historic remnants from the Mormon reign, the exhausted couple drove down to the boat dock. They parked the jeep, and sat quietly on a white wooden bench, watching the distant horizon erupt into a blaze of fiery oranges, purples and reds. The Beaver Island Lighthouse stood prominently in the distance. In a flash of time they saw the rising moon. One of the crew members of the docked, black and white Beaver Islander ferry boat, gestured to the passengers to come on board.

They heard the long, deep bellow of the last ferry boat back to Charlevoix.

CHAPTER 20

HISTORY OF THE QUIET LOON GOLF AND GUN CLUB

In 1925, a wealthy mining magnate by the name of Wilbur Randolph who was from Chicago needed a place halfway between Chicago and his Upper Peninsula mining interest so he could hide his mistress. Originally, he built an old log lodge on this site, which met his recreational needs. This was a private club and the members realized that they needed to cooperate with each other in order for the club to survive. The club cannot exist as either a gun club or golf club. He was always the capitalist entrepreneur and invited his wealthy Chicago friends up to the lodge. He started a skeet shooting range on the property when his golfing guests complained about the shotgun noise from the back lawn. It was a private club, but you had to have both activities for the private club to continue to exist. The two groups were always at odds with each other. Even their wives at the local market avoided each other.

It was down on its heels now in 1963. The present club officials considered the annual banquet a success if it didn't end in litigation. The skeet shooters thought it was great fun to use range balls as targets. In the past, the president of the East Jordan Banking and Trust Company considered it an honor to be president of this club. Recently, the local pizza parlor owner, Bob Smith was offered the position of president at the club and declined.

He said, "I am quartermaster at the local muskrat lodge. I need to order new hats for the 4th of July parade. We have a flea issue. I have a lot on my plate. The fezzes have fleas."

CHAPTER 21

THE 4th OF JULY PARADE

A highlight of the East Jordan summer season was the 4th of July Parade. Horton Bay had its tongue-in-cheek Bridge Walk and Charlevoix had its professionally scripted parade extravaganza, but East Jordan prided itself on its good old-fashioned 4th of July parade. The first parade was the brainchild of law and order Sheriff Bob Smithfield, who never missed an opportunity to campaign for re-election. The parade quickly became known locally as the "Bob Smithfield Re-election and Campaign Fundraising Parade." In early years, the parade was lucky to last for fifteen minutes. The joke among locals was that if you blinked, you missed it. However, over the years, it gradually became de rigueur to participate and the parade grew to over an hour in length. A Kiwanis BBQ chicken dinner, a carnival midway, a bake sale, bingo and a moonlight square dance rounded out a full day of activities.

New Whispering Pines owner, Maggie Sanders was determined to take full advantage of the free publicity, which the parade afforded. She envisioned a float, handcrafted by local artisans, which reflected the splendor of Whispering Pines, in all its glory.

She dreamed that the float would delight the crowd and wow the parade Judges. 1ˢᵗ Place in Float Design and Execution for 1963 was hers for the taking. Maggie dutifully filed her float application in early May and was proud when her float concept, a replica of the Whispering Pines, was approved by the Float Committee.

She immediately called a meeting of her "Top people," including Burt, Louie and Harry. She described her vision in detail to her team. She gave them carte blanche to buy and do whatever necessary (within reason) to bring her dream to fruition.

The morning of the 4ᵗʰ of July arrived hot, humid and sticky. The temperature crept above 80 degrees by nine o'clock as Maggie rushed to downtown East Jordan to stake out a prime spot along the parade route. She waited with anticipation. The parade commenced with the singing of "America the Beautiful" and a 1963 Plymouth Fury police car escort followed by a Military Color Guard.

Maggie repeatedly glanced far up the parade route looking for the Whispering Pines float to come into view. Finally, she recognized Burt's pick-up. Her heart raced as the float drew nearer. Exuberance turned to horror as she spotted the float. Her jaw dropped and her eyes popped as she watched the outhouse pass by. The door opened displaying Louie, decked out in a red velvet kings cape, gold crown and holding a scepter, perched on the throne waving to the crowd. Emblazoned on the side of the float was the slogan, "Too pooped to participate." People pointed and laughed hysterically. She hung her head and slinked away. All she could think of was her old shanty/outhouse days had come back to haunt her. It looked like she wasn't forgiven.

Dick, one of the new guests at the Inn, was sitting in a yellow and white webbed lawn chair along the parade route. This guy could get in trouble in church. He brought his Pop up Coleman camper to the Inn and liked to fall asleep in it after drinking a few beers.

He recently told Burt, "I just had to get away from the rat race."

Parade participants included the usual cast of characters living up to their promises.

Local politicians in bright red convertibles, church groups and area retailers were in abundance. A couple of Model T's appeared after a year's hibernation. Surrounding villages sent their prom queens, waving mechanically with their arms cocked at a 90-degree angle and wrist rotating. Upon close inspection, Miss Boyne City appeared a little green in the gills. A late night skinny-dipping escapade, by an inappropriate excess of Bali Hai, had had its lingering effect. Large quantities of water and Alka Seltzer made little appreciable difference. A thick layer of pancake make-up, haphazardly applied, actually gave her a Martian-like appearance.

Her stylish bouffant hairdo listed to one side, like a quickly melting dairy queen cone. "Just don't vomit. Just don't vomit," she kept telling herself.

The local Spiritualist Camp was faithfully represented by a menagerie of lost souls and seekers (of what, even they weren't sure). Each year farmer Ed Collins paraded with his collection of Allis Chalmers tractors and Dave Davis countered with his collection of Massey Fergusons. Bobbie Lee Turnbull showed off his fleet of three Kenworth's and one Peterbilt, horns glaring.

Rufus, the prize-winning steer, had been banned from the parade. His temperamental behavior had finally got the better of him the previous year. Rufus had broken loose from his tether, searched and found a comely sow and attempted crimes against nature. Although the local high school kids were captivated by the performance, the parade committee was not amused. Rufus's owner Elmer Quonset, reveled in his spirited steer's misconduct as Rufus's stud fee doubled.

The local dance studio, the Leapin Leotards, proudly paraded on a flatbed trailer, dancing enthusiastically to rock 'n roll hits like the "Wah-Watusi," "Peppermint Twist," and "The Locomotion." A sweaty Elvis impersonator, Tommy Albright, in a too tight silver jumpsuit, added a certain panache to the dance studio's performance. Elvis, the studio owner's husband, loosened up and decided to incorporate some leaps and splits into his routine. He soon regretted this decision as he heard the buttocks seam of his jumpsuit rip wide open. He spent the rest of the parade sitting on the flatbed throwing out candy to the kids.

A highlight of the parade was Dave Carter, the organist from the United Methodist Church. His Wurlitzer organ was mounted on a hay wagon pulled by a green, John Deere riding lawnmower driven by Leo Sturtevant. Mr. Sturtevant could not stand organ music; in fact, he loathed it.

Yet, each year he found himself coerced into pulling Dave Carter and his organ around town. The remainder of the year the two did not speak to each other and, truth be told, they did not speak to each other on the 4th of July. Organist Carter's repertoire consisted of five hymns, "Onward Christian Soldiers," "Holy, Holy, Holy," "Nearer My God to Thee," "How Great Thou Art" and "Amazing Grace." He added "Anchors Away" because it was a crowd pleaser. He always played these same six pieces whether at a wedding, funeral, church service or concert.

This year, Dave decided to expand his musical repertoire and added "Night Train" by James Brown. Rose Johnson's husband, Jim, accompanied him on his saxophone. The crowd applauded. Buzzing and astonished whispering swept through the crowd.

Leo Sturtevant dealt with the insufferable organ noise by adjusting his lawnmower carburetor so that it rumbled and drowned out the music. Mr. Carter's organ seemed to always be positioned behind the 4 H Equestrian Club. It was hard for the organist to focus with the strong odor of horse manure wafting in the air and his driver, Leo, constantly swerving to avoid a minefield of horseshit.

Dave retained his dignity and calmly played until the parade ended on Main Street.

CHAPTER 22

JOHANNA VISITS THE HAIR HUT

"Another day, another dollar, or shall I say another unusual rock formation," Johanna thought ruefully as she walked out to her green and white, 1960 Willys Jeep station wagon for another day of rock hunting. Halfway there, she plopped herself onto a yellow and green webbed lawn chair, leaned her head up toward the sky and closed her eyes.

"What am I doing here?" she thought.

Roberta, the main housekeeper at the Inn, who lived in a small frame house outside Charlevoix, arrived for work a little late and approached Johanna tentatively and then quietly asked, "A penny for your thoughts?"

Johanna opened her eyes and asked, "Do you think I'm pretty? I mean not handsome or statuesque or cute for my age, but actually pretty. I don't feel pretty."

"You're a very beautiful woman," Roberta said. "You just try so hard to hide it."

"I don't try to. I guess it comes with the territory...U. P. native, mining professor and all that implies."

Roberta thought for a moment and then said, "Follow me. I

have a plan." Roberta hurried off and returned shortly driving a 1954 rusted out blue Chevy Bel Air. She swung open the passenger door. "C'mon. We're going to the Hair Hut. You're getting a make-over," Roberta declared.

The Hair Hut was aptly named. The beauty establishment was an appendage tacked onto the side of an old white frame farm-house. The only identification it had was a lime green plywood sign nailed onto a fence post at the end of the gravel driveway.

"You're lucky Peggy could fit you in. I had to pull some strings," Roberta said.

Observing that there were no other cars parked in the vicinity, Johanna had her doubts but, as strings had been pulled, there was no backing out now.

The inside of the Hair Hut consisted of two, powder blue Naugahyde barber's chairs, a sink and mirror, beautician's work station and two black, beehive hair dryer chairs. The odor of hair permanent chemicals permeated the air. The black clock on the wall said twelve o'clock.

"Don't you worry. You're in Peggy's hands now," said Peggy, beautician/owner in residence. When Johanna got a really good look at Peggy, she began to worry. Peggy had a messy beehive hair-do, large loop earrings and wore thick, black eyeliner with, black, drawn on eyebrows that arched a little higher than they should. It was not at all unusual to be waited on by the owner in one of the town's customer friendly businesses, but first impressions of her ability to judge what it means to be well-groomed did not bode well.

Roberta attempted to tell Peggy what she felt Johanna needed. "Stop right there," Peggy commanded. "I have a vision."

"See you gals later," Roberta said.

Peggy turned her full attention to Johanna. "I have Fanta, 7-Up or Coca-Cola, if you're thirsty." She guided Johanna to the barber's chair, gowned her, tipped her back, and raised her up with a few pumps of the barber chair's lever. Peggy was in the zone. She was totally focused and concentrated all of her energy into creating a new look for Johanna, one she would never forget. Johanna relaxed and put all of her trust in Peggy and her skills with hair. Johanna left all of her emotional baggage behind her for the day. She let out a long, deep sigh...she was dozing.

Peggy suddenly got very busy. Miss Boyne City rushed in and took a deep breath through her nose. "I need a new do!" "You will never believe what happened to me at the parade yesterday!"

"People were pointing their fingers and laughing at me through the entire parade!" she exclaimed.

"I am sure they were laughing with you dear, not at you," Peggy told her, trying to calm her down.

Peggy offered the beauty queen a hot cup of fresh coffee. Miss Boyne City was the daughter of Stanley Newman, one of the most prominent members of the East Jordan community. Peggy took great pride in providing prompt customer service and realized her opportunity to elevate herself in the eyes of the community. Peggy worked on Miss Newman for over an hour and a half and forgot all about Johanna.

Later, around 1:45 P.M., the beautification renovation project was complete. Hair, nails, makeup, the whole shebang. Peggy offered Johanna a large mirror.

Johanna hesitated, then held up the mirror and let out a gasp of surprise. "I know," said Peggy. "It's better than I could imagine."

Johanna surveyed the damage. Her once beautiful, auburn hair now had rusty red highlights. It cascaded upward into a frenzied bouffant. Animals would find it an ideal nesting place. Her makeup called to mind a Marseille street walker.

The nails were a haphazard afterthought, at best. Unbelievably, Peggy had forgotten to file and polish the nail on the pinky finger of Johanna's left hand. Johanna did not care to remind her.

Mirror in hand, Johanna continued to survey the damage. "I know," exclaimed Peggy. "Isn't it spectacular? And the best thing, dear, you get the new customer discount."

BEAVER ISLAND – A LITTLE PIECE OF HEAVEN
1963

Burt had his eye on Maggie forever. He was increasingly suspicious of Chef Claude as of late.

Recently, Claude said, "Look Burt, Maggie needs a break!"

Burt told Maggie some friends of theirs were going to meet them on Beaver Island for the day. She agreed to go. Come to find out, the friends couldn't make it to the Island. Leo and Penny Sullivan owned one of the few vineyards in the area, and unfortunately that same day, were viciously attacked by wasps from a large wasp nest situated near their garden. They both ended up in the hospital for multiple wasps stings all over their bodies.

It was a cool, sunny day in early July. The deep blue sky was cloudless. Burt was convinced that a change of scenery and the charm of Beaver Island would provide a haven where Maggie could relax and find herself again.

They took the ferry and borrowed a Jeep once they arrived on the Island. Maggie took the wheel. Maggie was trying to run the show but she had never been on the Island so they got lost. All of a sudden, after driving for hours, they found themselves on a beautiful lake. Burt had packed a nap sack with a telescoping travel fishing rod. He caught some pan fish and grilled a shore lunch.

Maggie enthusiastically pointed out, "This is the best fish I ever tasted!"

Burt asked, "Better than Chef Claude's?"

"Yes, Burt."

Then Maggie said, "We better get going."

Burt drove straight to the dock but they had missed the last ferry boat to Charlevoix. Burt and Maggie walked over to the only bar and restaurant on the Island and inquired about renting a room for the night.

They were referred to a rooming house a few blocks away. Maggie was mad at first, and accused Burt of planning the entire weekend.

"And I suppose you brought your toothbrush?" Maggie said sarcastically.

Burt chuckled.

To calm her, Burt pulled up in front of the Five and Dime and handed her a $20.00 bill to get whatever she wanted.

A little after midnight, Burt said, "I am sorry Maggie for the way things turned out today. I hope you forgive me."

"Yes, Burt, I forgive you," she said.

"You know Maggie, I really miss your kisses," Burt chimed in.

"You don't miss me-just my kisses?" she interjected.

"Time to start faking," Burt chortled.

He was very sweet and charming and she couldn't help wondering about her feelings of love now that were so unexpected. In retrospect, it was obvious that she must have loved Burt for a very long time, but denied it to herself. Burt went to sleep on the sofa.

They woke up on Sunday to the bright sun shining through the sheer white drapes and the sound of waves lapping against the shore, seagull cries and relaxed tourists laughing. What they didn't know was 25 foot waves and high winds had hit Lake Michigan. They boarded the ferry back to Charlevoix. The atmosphere was one of excitement and spontaneity among the fellow passengers. Maggie adopted a persona of being angry and upset for the entire trip but actually had a really good time. On the ferry, she gave Burt the cold shoulder trying to send the message that once they were back on the mainland, nothing had changed in their relationship.

During the trip across Lake Michigan, she watched the coolers strapped onto the deck railing loosen and finally break loose. The coolers tipped over disgorging their contents. She became mesmerized watching all the trash fly from one side of the deck to the other. All of it flew overboard eventually.

Burt gasped when a six-pack of Schlitz slid across the deck and disappeared.

Maggie's mind drifted back to the Inn and all the problems she would face come tomorrow morning, "If only my worries could be washed overboard just like this trash," she thought.

"Maybe I can start fresh, somewhere, somehow."

Burt moved closer to her on the dark blue bench seat, reached out and held her hand.

"Don't worry he said, I'm here to help you get through this."

"Through what?" she thought. "This trip or this season? Had Burt read her mind?"

HARRY, ROBERTA AND SUNSET HILL

The next day, Roberta heard all about Maggie's trip to Beaver Island. She walked over to the back of the Inn where Harry was trimming Maple trees. He was lost in his own world, thinking about what he had heard from Burt about the "Christmas Tree Trimmers," and the impression they had made on everyone at the Chat and Chew. "I wonder if I could lure some of them over here to help me with the promise of mom's famous mash potatoes and fresh black coffee," Harry pondered.

Just at that moment, Roberta started ragging Harry's ass-"You never take me anywhere exciting!"

Harry, a little startled said, "I had no idea this was so important to you. C'mon, I'll take you up to Sunset Hill, up in the hills between Charlevoix and Petoskey."

Roberta shrugged. "Oh how romantic, you mean where all the high school kids go?"

Being in a lighthearted mood and trying to reassure her Harry said, "I got my own Sunset Hill. We can pick up fresh strawberries from Ella's fruit and vegetable stand on the way. I have an old Army blanket just in case it gets cold later."

They hopped in his car and Harry turned the radio dial to WRAM 009 AM. Fats Domino was singing, "I Found My Thrill on Blueberry Hill."

Roberta started to feel flirtatious.

She snuggled up to Harry and inquired, "How much further?"

Harry, deeply moved by her gesture said, "I can't go too fast, it's kind of bumpy." "Hang on!"

On the way up the hill, the car got stuck in the sand. This was the hill Harry claimed to know so well. It was all overgrown; worse than he remembered. He was so proud that he had the winch to pull them out of the sand. But he always came prepared and even had a beige, homemade mosquito net head cover for Roberta for protection while he continued to crank the winch and eventually pull the car out of the sand.

As the sun faded away behind the white pine trees, Roberta stood quietly and then said, "Harry, let's go to my place," as she slapped a mosquito off her neck.

"Now that is the deepest desire of my heart," thought Harry.

CHAPTER 23

LOCKED AND LOADED

Burt did not show up for work at 8 A. M., at 9 A.M., at 10:30 A.M. The black rotary phone on his nightstand began ringing incessantly. If Burt had still carried a pistol, he would have shot that infernal device to bits and pieces. Burt dragged himself over to Maggie's office at one o'clock.

"Has little Lord Fauntleroy decided to play some cricket or perhaps there's a polo match this afternoon?" Maggie piped up.

"Come rest, let me get you a beverage as the walk from the parking lot to my office must have left you simply parched."

"Where do you get off talking to me like that, Maggie? I was sick. I am sick but I'm here now. So what do you want me to do?" Burt replied.

"Here's the work orders. You figure it out," Maggie snapped.

Burt enlisted in the Navy in 1941 at the age of 22. While he was serving his country on Saipan Island in the western Pacific, he contracted malaria. Malaria is a pernicious disease that lingers in the blood stream until death. Some patients experience no symptoms after the first onset. Others are plagued by recurrent symptoms throughout the remainder of their life. These symptoms may include: night sweats, fever, fatigue, and muscle soreness. Symptoms may be mild or seriously debilitating. Burt's Malaria was mild but unpredictable during the majority of episodes and occasionally disabling.

Today, July 10, 1963 was one of those days.

"I told you a few days ago that the refrigerator in the kitchen needs a new thermostat from cooling & refrigeration experts at Because You Can't Wait Appliance Store in Traverse City," Maggie continued.

"You told me I had better things to do," Burt sighed.

Maggie says, "And by the way… I need that trash outta here now!"

Burt was given his marching orders.

Burt stormed off, heading to the dump. He had no business showing up to work to begin with. He still had a 100 degree temperature and chills. "I should be in bed," Burt thought to himself.

"I hustled my ass just to get in here and she treats me like that!"

Burt, determined as he was, surveyed the parking lot and realized the old green Studebaker truck was gone. Louie was God only knew where, doing God only knows what.

"She wants the trash out of here, I'll get it out of here," Burt told himself.

He went directly to the garage and took the car keys to Maggie's 1959, yellow Ford station wagon. For the next thirty minutes, he began at the kitchen back door and loaded seven heavy bags of kitchen refuse into the back seat of the wagon.

Then he made his rounds to the laundry and housekeeping and outdoor receptacles. Soon the station wagon was full. Even the front passenger seat held a couple of bags of trash. After shoving one final bag of trash into the wagon, Burt slammed the door shut and stepped back to check his work. He drove the wagon up to the office entrance and parked.

"I will let this marinate for a while before I take it to the dump. So many work orders, so little time," Burt chuckled to himself.

INTERCOM PROBLEMS

Later that day, Maggie tried to locate Burt through the intercom system. The labels were half off, coming off, buttons were mislabeled, it screeched, it was stat icky.

Burt stood in the door way and said, "Were you looking for me?"

Maggie stared at Burt, "This damn intercom, why isn't it fixed?"

"I seem to recall trouble shooting the intercom back in April, but I will need help from Bob to fix it properly," Burt answered.

Half grinning, Maggie softened and said, "All right Burt, I trust that you two will perform something miraculous."

"By the way Burt, I am sorry if I caused you any anguish earlier today. I am exhausted. I have been working over 18 hours straight, every day, trying to get a handle on maintenance issues around here." Burt felt his heart melt and maybe a little regret for leaving the trash in her car earlier.

LOUIE AND THE LAWNMOWER
JULY 1963

Louie was a lost soul and drove Burt nuts with his antics and abuse of the Inn's equipment. He had no common sense.

Louie rose to the 6:30 A. M. clang of the Big Ben. He stretched, scratched, and hit the can. Splashing water on his face, he squeezed some Brylcreem onto his scalp, rubbed it in and combed back his long black hair into a greaser pompadour. He then critically perused what God had wrought and smiled at what he saw. He liked to believe he was a legend in his own lifetime. All was well in Louie land. He returned to the living room/bedroom of the cabin and poured a bitter cup of coffee from his old stainless steel percolator into a stained EJIW coffee mug. He sipped the coffee with pleasure and reassured himself that he was not living on a defunct dude ranch.

Louie now began his morning dressage. He cued up Jerry Lee Lewis on his See burg 1000 phonograph. The driving beat filled the room. Bopping to the Killer's pounding piano, Louie slipped into a pair of black jeans and a tight fitting short sleeved t-shirt. Over the jeans he strapped on a pair of black leather chaps. He donned a black leather Harley-Davidson vest. Sitting on the edge of his bed, Louie pulled on some heavy white socks and a pair of black, steel toed Harley-Davidson motorcycle boots. He synched the laces extra tight.

He stood up, gulped down the rest of his coffee and still jerking spastically to Jerry Lee's throbbing piano, spun around to check things out in the full length mirror hanging on the bathroom door. "Yeah," he thought. "That's one bad ass mother."

He completed his ensemble by donning a black dew rag, followed by a pair of blue tinted sunglasses and a bicycle helmet.

Louie emerged and mounted his stead tethered near the side of the cabin.

With a cigarette hanging out of his mouth, he strapped himself into the racing seat and fired up the ignition. The beast immediately roared to life. With a few gooses of the throttle, the powerful machine belched out loud, low rumbles. Louie let the monster idle as he ran through his checklist and checked if anyone had noticed his performance. He threw the mower into forward and lurched into the parking lot, spewing a cloud of dust and gravel. Louie's day had begun.

CHAPTER 24

LOUIE'S SHUTTLE SERVICE

From the Belvedere Club, take Belvedere Avenue to Bridge Street (U.S.31), turn left, go to Highway 66, turn left and go about two miles to Castle Farm.

After the Whispering Pines' Fourth of July debacle, Maggie needed a lift.

Burt was happy to report the white VW bus was up and running. Some basic mechanical repairs, courtesy of Bob, and a thorough scrubbing had transformed the van into a respectable transportation vehicle. Maggie inspected Burt's handiwork and even she had to grudgingly admit that it didn't look bad. Now the Whispering Pines could provide shuttle service for guests flying into Charlevoix and thereby compete with the fancy schmancy resorts of Charlevoix and Petoskey.

By default, Louie was assigned transport duty. "At least, it gets him out of here for a while," Maggie reasoned. In contrast, Louie considered his new responsibility a promotion. "At last, somebody is recognizing my worth," he thought to himself. He viewed himself as a guy with infinite charm and personality. Full of youthfulness and illusions, Louie was determined to milk his opportunity for all it was worth.

He soon developed a repertoire of tour guide banter or a slurry of sightseeing points of interest, local history and folklore. He practiced this spiel in front of his mirror for several nights.

Maggie walked by his cabin one night and overheard a snippet of his oration. "Oh, no! What have I done?" she asked herself. "I don't want to know," she answered.

The inaugural shuttle service kicked off on a hot, humid July afternoon in 1963. About 3:00 P.M. Chef Claude stood outside taking a smoke break, when the shuttle arrived. He watched with growing interest as Inn guests disembarked in various stages of dishevelment. Expressions ranged from amusement to shock. One older couple was visibly shaken. The husband guided his wife into the nearest Adirondack chair and rushed into the lobby to get her a glass of water. A middle-aged couple appeared giddy with laughter. Chef offered complimentary Sherry to the guests to Maggie's dismay. "How much is this gonna cost me?" she asked him sarcastically.

Chef feared that the shuttle service, under Louie's control, could better be described as "Mr. Toad's Wild Ride." He decided he better check things out.

The next day, assistant cook Sally hitched a ride to Charlevoix on the pretext of buying some parsley. In truth, she was assigned a reconnaissance mission with a sitrep to be delivered to Chef if and when she returned.

Late afternoon, the van was seen racing through the parking lot and screeching to an abrupt halt before the Inn's main entrance. Sally rushed to Chef, excited and breathless. "Holy shit. You would not believe what I just lived through," she exclaimed.

Sally then proceeded to give Chef a minute-by-minute account of her trip through hell.

"Getting there, Louie drove way too fast. He forgot to drop me off, whizzed right by Osborn's Grocery Store and didn't stop until he was on the airport runway. Suddenly, I heard a loud voice from the control tower order the van off the runway and onto the grass. Not a moment too soon, either.

Seconds later a blue and white 20 passenger turboprop flew just over our heads and landed on the very same runway we had just exited. At this point, airport security blocked us with two Jeeps. Four security guards surrounded our vehicle, holsters unlatched.

Louie's idiotic explanation made no sense whatsoever, but did convince the officers that his confusion was innocent.

When we eventually located the plane carrying our Inn guests, I quickly realized that they had witnessed the entire drama. They slowly filed into the VW van with obvious trepidation and suspicious looks on their faces."

"Before we started moving," Sally continued, "Louie grew bolder with each passing minute." Louie's mind wasn't engaged in the antics swirling around him.

"I am confident that you are not aware of the stunning history I am going to impart to you today," he said.

Louie leapt to his feet, "Let me begin by saying that Castle Farms was built by the Loeb family back in 1918."

"It was modeled after the stone barns and castles found in Normandy, France," Louie stated with a voice of authority.

What Louie did next was try to spin a web of images of the events and people tied to the Leopold and Loeb Trial, which was known as the "Crime of the Century."

Louie shared his impassioned historical insights about the famous crime with the group.

"The trouble began when Leopold and Loeb met while living in Chicago during the early 1920's," said Louie.

"You see, Leopold[10] had an unquenchable obsession with the

---

10 "He would talk endlessly about the mythical superman who, because he was a superman, stood outside the law, beyond any moral code that might constrain

philosophy of Friedrich Nietzsche."

Louie proceeds to read his notes to the group who were all ears now.

"Leopold was, moreover, agreeable to Loeb's plan to kidnap a child," Louie said. Louie spoke eloquently because he was committed to describing the horrible crime in detail.

"Oh my God," one lady sighed.

Louie always felt disappointed when he witnessed people hardly noticing him or worse yet, not listening to him. This day was different. Louie was very excited, for now he had his big opportunity to hone his public speaking skills and gain the recognition he felt he deserved.

"Just wait, there is more!" Louie said. Wide eyed, they all are invested now and waited patiently for the remainder of the story to be delivered. It was almost too much to absorb.

Louie cleared his throat and proceeded to read an article from the Petoskey News:

> *"World renowned defense attorney Clarence Darrow spent a few days in Northern Michigan in 1924 while conducting background and character research on Richard Loeb and Nathan Leopold, summer resorter's in Charlevoix.*
>
> *Young Leopold and Loeb had been charged with the murder of the boy Bobby Franks in Chicago. The pair were carrying out one of Loeb's fantasies--to commit the perfect crime.*
>
> *Darrow, the famed "Attorney for the Damned," was hired to defend the boys, because Darrow was an eloquent foe of capital punishment. Richard Loeb's father was the owner of Sears &*

the actions of ordinary men. Even murder, Leopold claimed, was an acceptable act for a superman to commit if the deed gave him pleasure. Morality did not apply in such a case."

Roebucks and Leopold's father was a renowned doctor.

The parents had great hopes for their paranormal prodigies, prior to the failed plot. The boys were so confident of their perfect crime that they led the police around giving tips on how to catch the culprits. But after Leopold's glasses were discovered in the river where Bobby Franks' body was found, they admitted their guilt."

-James Vol Hartwell, (Petoskey: The Petoskey News, 2011)

"Chef, Louie held the attention of the guests for over 30 minutes while he spoke of the dark history regarding the Loeb family and the crime of the Century," said Sally.

"Well, once you got back on the road, things turned out OK?" Chef asked.

"No. That's when the troubles began," Sally replied.

"Full of moxie, Louie gunned the VW and lurched over the field and through a service exit. After a series of zigs and zags we found ourselves on U.S. 131 heading south toward Traverse City. I didn't want to say anything because Louie seemed totally out of it. He calmed down after a while and that's when I hoped I'd get him turned around, heading back in the right direction. Not stopping, that's when he went off the road."

"What?"

"Yeah," Sally continued. "He went off the road. South of Charlevoix, past the Medusa Cement turnoff, where U.S. 131 narrows back down to one lane. Well, Louie was in the right lane and he kept driving in the right lane but there was no right lane. He was driving along 60 miles an hour on the shoulder. Then the shoulder narrowed and he kept driving right along over sand and patches of grass. He was completely oblivious.

He even changed stations on the radio. The van bounced along like it had a flat. Everybody looked at each other but no one was brave enough to speak up.

Right about then I looked back at the guests, nonchalant like, pretending everything was under control. When I turned back around there it was, dead center right in our path, a row of mail-boxes and Louie driving along happy as could be."

"Louie, watch out!" I screamed. "He swerved, missed them and came to a stop."

"Damn mailboxes! Right in front of me. Somebody needs to do something," Louie snapped.

"Well, I got Louie headed over to the Inn through Ellsworth. No more excitement. We made it," Sally sighed.

TRADITION

Fishermen had always been keenly aware of the moods of the lakes surrounding Charlevoix County. It was difficult to imagine the resort community of East Jordan without its heritage of forests and spectacular lakes.

There was a tradition up north, and it proved to be irresistible to the fishermen who knew about it. Four local farms owned little lakes and the farmers kept an old coffee can on each of the back porches with a slit on top for the $2.00 the fishermen would have to pay to fish. To seize the moment, fishermen would pick up their oars out of the farmers sheds and head down to the lake for a day of fishing. They would fish for blue gills, perch, and sunfish and late at dusk could always catch a nice bass by the Lilly pads. One farmer named Al, had a big, vicious dog named Harley, whose favorite snack was a fisherman.

The men would have to drive the car right up to the shed. One person would divert the attention of the dog. The other person would grab the oars and place them sideways into the car. Then the driver would take off like a bat out of hell. The dog would leave slime and paw prints all over the driver's side window as they took off.

One of the fishermen exclaimed, "That was a pleasant interlude!"

Northern Michigan supplied the fishermen with no less than ten lake trout each, a catch fit for a King. Their laughter carried over the water, as the daylong brightness of the sun and their success reignited their passion for fishing.

BILL

There was a guy named Bill who lived at the Inn every summer and fall. 1963 was no exception. Bill never tired of looking up at the stars that glimmered palely in the black sky and listening to the water washing backward and forward against the shore. During the winter months, Bill retreated to the simplicity and tranquility of Beaver Island. There, he lived in an old, green mobile home situated on two acres down Barneys Lake Road. Weathered barns, log houses, aged apple orchards, clapboard buildings with high false fronts and posted business hours signs followed by the words "weather permitting" were all part of the island's rustic charm. The island had its share of fascinating, educated, worldly, creative, and resilient individuals who had chosen a simpler and quieter way of life and Bill was one of them.

Bill was a professional fisherman or in other words, he earned his living fishing. Bill was a fun kind of guy with lots of entertaining antidotes, provided free of charge to anyone who would listen. A moral, intelligent, and articulate man with long brown hair and

a moustache, badly in need of a trim, Bill lived a simple and mini-
malist life in the Northern woods. Bill was greatly loved and ad-
mired by all of the local people. Bill was also a philosopher. Usually
he was quiet and pretty much kept to himself. Nobody knew him
that well. Today was different and he shared some wisdom with
Burt. Burt asked Bill, "Do you think the fish feel any pain?" Bill
answered him, "Of course and we need not be nostalgic about animal suffering; but we dare not be cruel or callous; fish do suffer."

Bill went on to say, "Life is suffering; but life is good. Animals
and humans wrestle for the life of their kind, and humans bear a
special testimony to the goodness of life by their undying hope of
a future life. Life involves suffering and mercy. Just like nature is
merciful. I have known great pain and suffered. Because of this I
see the pain as a blessing in disguise, an anodyne and a gift of life."

People would often ask him, "Where are the fish biting today
Bill?" to which he would answer, "Hum, I think I need to find out
which way the wind is blowing."

When asked, "What fishing spots are you familiar with?" Bill
responded, "Chester's Landing, Dave's Dry Dock, Sam's Swamp,
Chad's Point and Leonard's Limestone Lake."

A week after Bill settled in, Burt walked by and noticed him
sitting on the porch of his cabin, softly singing to himself a Henry Thomas, "Ragtime Texas" ditty, "Fishing Blues." Bill had his
hands full, cleaning trout that he just caught that morning. Burt
was hooked.

The next day, Bill headed down to the dock, with Burt in tow
and fishing pole and tackle box in hand.

Bill, being full of a lot of hot air, told Burt a story he had picked
up during his adventurous life as a fisherman, "A guy went five
miles out on Lake Michigan in the middle of the winter, 1950. He
was icebound, along with his best friend.

He called the Coast Guard and they asked, "Is your life in peril?"

The guy said, "No, but we can't move."

"Well, call us when your life is in peril," replied the Coast Guard.

The fishermen passed around a fifth of Jack and then they started goosing the boat forward and backwards. It took an hour to turn the boat 180 degrees and finally they returned to the harbor in Charlevoix.

After this incident, the guy said to himself, "There has to be an easier way to make a living."

His comrade said, "Yeah, you better find another guy to get us the next bottle of Jack. I am not setting foot on a boat ever again."

FISH OR CUT BAIT

Burt kept thinking to himself, "How did things get so complicated?"

He signed on as General Manager back in the winter, when Maggie inherited the Inn. He had visions of working with Maggie as a team, side by side, bringing the Whispering Pines back to some semblance of its heyday and in the process reconnecting with Maggie and sweeping her off her feet. But somewhere things went wrong. The job was too big or maybe the task was too unrealistic. And Burt and Maggie too old.

Burt liked to reminiscence about the ways things once were when he was young and carefree and having fun with Maggie out on the water. Skinny dipping, and floating on Lake Charlevoix at night using a spotlight to spot fish were a couple of his favorites. Sitting around a bonfire telling ghost stories held his interest. Pulling pranks, skipping school, driving around, listening to the radio and songs like "Goodnight My Love" sung by Sarah Vaughan.

Burt thought to himself, "I'm going to hang in there for a while longer. Finish out the tourist season. Then see where things are at. I can't do this much longer."

CHAPTER 25

THE RISOTTO
JULY 1963

Chef Claude was happiest when he was in his kitchen at the Inn. "Aaargh!! Andrea!"

Chef slammed the scorched pot down on the South Bend cooktop. He turned, scanning the kitchen for the guilty culprit. No luck. He stared again into the disgusting pot of burnt glop.

The acrid stench of charred rice filled the room. A beautiful risotto...ruined. Chef circled the kitchen, furious. Still no Andrea. Cooks busied themselves at their workstations, heads down, snatching furtive glances, sharing grimaces, grins.

"I'll go find her," the Sous-Chef finally said.

Andrea was on a smoke break. Andrea didn't smoke. At least, not any more. Andrea didn't smoke because it was gross. It made her breath and hair smell bad. Mick said so. But Andrea still took smoke breaks. It just wouldn't be fair if she didn't.

"Mick is totally sick. So laid back, so deep. And can that boy stroll a pair of Levi's jeans," Andrea thought.

Andrea got a ride to work with Mick. That way if she wanted to hang out with him later on she could ask him for a ride home.

Unless he ditched her and he had ditched her. But she'd heard talk about the cooks going out after work. If they went out, Andrea would go and then Mick would come too. But she didn't trust those girls around Mick or was it she didn't trust Mick around those girls. She hit the candy machine and out popped a box of good and plenty.

"Anywhoo…" Andrea's reverie was interrupted when the back door opened and a sliver of light illuminated the loading dock.

"Andrea. Chef," a voice urgently called.

"Oh no! The risotto."

Risotto is not a food. It is not an ingredient. It is not a grain, a legume, a starch or a vegetable. Risotto is a dish made from short-grained rice. Classic risotto recipes include wild mushroom risotto, asparagus risotto and Parmigiano-Reggiano risotto. There is no hidden formula to making a good risotto. Recipes are remarkably similar. The only secret to constructing a good risotto is time and patience. At the critical moment in preparation, hot stock is added to the rice, in small increments, and the rice is stirred, gently and steadily, for over twenty minutes. One cannot hurry a risotto. One cannot neglect a risotto. A risotto requires tender, loving care. A properly made risotto transforms simple ingredients into a rich, creamy, culinary masterpiece.

"What am I going to do with that young lady?" Chef wondered. Andrea was scatterbrained, impulsive, and unpredictable. She was also curious, hardworking, vivacious and charismatic. When she was on, she was on. "I've got to be strong. I've got to set an example," Chef told himself. Then he remembered the night the grill cook never showed up. Not the first time. "Don't worry. I got this," Andrea had boasted.

"What other choice do I have?" Chef thought.

Tentative at first, Andrea quickly got up to speed. Finding her way. The steaks, the chops, the char-grilled salmon, the tickets all went out, on time, and, miraculously, didn't come back. With the kitchen in the weeds, Chef actually caught himself, shaking his head in disbelief, watching Andrea rockin' the grill, workin' hard, having fun.

At one point, a waiter popped his head into the kitchen. "The six top had steaks and send their compliments to the Chef," he said. Andrea gave a little fist pump and turned from side to side, nodding her head, letting the kitchen know "king of the grill in the house."

"Oh my goodness. There's something there," Chef had thought.

Chef watched Andrea skulk back into the kitchen and saw himself, thirty-five years younger. Just a kid, still a lot of mistakes to wash down the drain. Andrea stood silently before Chef. Chef thrust the smoldering pot of risotto in Andrea's face.

"Oh wow. You really do have to stir it."

Andrea's eyes met Chef's. "I'm so sorry. I've learned my lesson. It won't happen again." Andrea's eyes pleaded.

"Start over," Chef barked.

"Yes, Chef," came Andrea's contrite reply.

"And clean this pot before you go home."

"Yes, Chef."

Chef turned, walked away and smiled.

CHAPTER 26

VENETIAN FESTIVAL

The Venetian Festival began in Charlevoix in 1930 when the Belvedere Club and the Chicago Club held a boat parade that circled around Round Lake. The festival started with a carnival midway, beach picnic, games, music at the Tiki Tent and a variety of food. It concluded with the Venetian Boat parade and fireworks. The city was a fashionable retreat for vacationers going back to the turn of the century.

Glancing at the antique clock on the wall in the café, Maggie noticed it was almost half-past nine. Maggie saw the flyer for the July 21, 1963 Venetian Festival posted in the Chat and Chew earlier that morning. She ran out to where her car was parked and sped back to the Inn.

Once there, the only person she could find was Johanna.

"Come on Johanna, what do you say we meander down to the Venetian Festival together?"

"Alright," Johanna answered with trepidation.

They arrived twenty minutes later in downtown Charlevoix. The weather was perfect, with the temperature at 75 degrees and a northerly wind.

The carnival midway just started at 10:00 A.M. The white side-walks of the city were lined with souvenir shops and cafés, while up Bridge Street you could see the double-leaf bascule bridge, which was dedicated as a memorial to 22 local men who died during World War II.

Fred Candleman was already walking around with his white ice cream cooler on wheels. Handmade flag pennant banners in colors of red, green, yellow and blue decorated the walkways. There were red and white checkered table cloths on tables with hot dogs, pizza and potato chips available to purchase. High school girls with lots of confidence invited passersby to buy snow cones and cotton candy. A Ferris wheel and a Tilt-A-Whirl each had a lineup of parents and children who were waiting to board. The squeals of thrill seekers rose above the chatter on the street, and could be heard off in the distance. There was an element of excitement in the air.

There was a row of booths with Kewpie dolls lined up inside. Louie was standing near one of the booths smoking a cigarette. He was going for a Knight Templar look. He wore black motorcycle boots, long johns, a plaid, loose shirt cinched at the waist, a black eye patch and a spray painted newspaper pirate hat. Some local high school kids walked passed him and said sarcastically, "Nice look, Louie."

To which Louie replied, "Put an egg in your shoe and beat it."

Wilma Adkins gave Louie the evil eye and gestured for him to come over to her. "You need to hurry over to the Gazebo on Park Street and run the Cake Walk show. Carmen Harrison is sick and I need you to replace her. All the squares with numbers, black top hat, record player with music, pieces of paper with numbers on them and baked goods in boxes from Marilyn's bakery are there," she insisted. Louie agreed to help.

Louie started off okay, but things got out of control when two children stopped on the same number and started screaming at him. Louie just happened to see Burt walking by and called out to him, "Burt, can you come and help me out here temporally?" Burt stepped up and took over. Louie asked, "In the spirit of community, can you give me a short break?"

Burt replied, "Sure, but come back!"

Burt knew instinctively that Louie would never come back and he was right.

Tony Bonedini, Township Supervisor, was the guy in the strong man carnival face cut out. Kids were lined up to throw water balloons at him. Tony was busy laughing and having a good time and he didn't realize the next person in line was his ex-wife, Jasmine. She started whipping tomatoes at him out of a grocery bag. "Hey," he yelled. "Make her stop that!"

A crowd soon gathered. Jasmine continued her bombardment. As a former all state softball pitcher, and MVP, her pitches hit the mark-Tony's face!

"Come on stop that!" Tony yelled.

"I'm just a makin' pasta sauce. Just lika your mama. It's a good," Jasmine said, kissing her fingers in a gesture of delight.

FIREMAN'S FIELD DAY

An annual event that took place just a few blocks away was the Fireman's Field Day. One of the highlights was the grease pole with a $5.00 bill tacked to the top. Maggie won it when she was a kid, and expected recognition, but the local boys who were humiliated shunned her.

They had a three legged sack race that required rhythm, a wheel barrel race where one person walked on their hands and the other held that persons legs, a shoe kick which involved who kicked their shoe the farthest, egg toss, 50 and 100 yard dash, pigeon rolling, penny scramble, and a jug hanging on a wire.

Harry and Roberta walked all around. Roberta seemed bored.

Wanting to impress Roberta, Harry, being a volunteer fireman, reached out his hand and said, "Come on, let me show you what a real fireman can do!"

They walked over to the Fireman's main field day event. On each end of the wire was a fireman. When the Fire Chief said, "Go!" they turned on the fire hoses and each team aimed the hoses at the jug. The jug went flying back and forth and the team that aimed their hose most accurately at the jug, shot the jug overhead past the other team and won. Roberta cheered for Harry and it turned out to be the one bright spot in his day.

VENETIAN BOAT PARADE

"There is nothing in a caterpillar that tells you it's going to be a butterfly."
-Buckminster Fuller

As the evening waned, Maggie and Johanna walked arm and arm as they strode downtown to the water's edge and stood with the on-lookers, waiting with anticipation for the boats to make their way around the lake.

They were becoming fast friends.

"Is that 'The Ride of the Valkyries' by Richard Wagner I hear coming from the Harbor Master patrol boat?" Johanna asked.

Maggie replied, "Yes, it's adding another dimension to the anticipation!"

Last year, the parade went counter clockwise, this year it was going clockwise, just to give people something to talk about. The lights on the boats were on the wrong side. Everyone was to follow the parade in reverse to disguise faux pas donuts. Boats rocked wildly and people grappled to keep their strings of white lights secure on their boats. Boisterous laughter and shouting was heard coming from most of the boats.

Johanna noticed a lady about 85 years old, wearing a blonde wig and dark pancake makeup. A guy yelled from another boat, "Surrender your wenches!" Maggie and Johanna thought she looked vaguely familiar.

The older lady yelled back, "Not this wench!"

They both turned around and realized it was Adeline.

Johanna wore a loose flowing white blouse that showed her ample breasts swaying freely, and a long flowing skirt. "My God" she thought, "this can only end badly but I haven't felt so alive in 20 years."

Being one of the resorters captivated by the beauty of Charlevoix, and the charms of Gus, Johanna just couldn't seem to get enough. Strolling along the waterfront, the sky ablaze with colors of fuchsia and yellow, Johanna was struck for a moment by Charlevoix's tranquility and breathtaking beauty.

GUS CAMPBELL

Gus invited Johanna over to his place for coffee and donuts the next day. When Gus stepped outside to talk to Burt about using one of the rowboats to take Johanna out on the lake, she noticed a chest of drawers in the corner of his cottage living room. She slipped off her flats, and curious, she opened it and found some military paraphernalia, a degree from Trinity College in Dublin, a black French beret and a photograph of a woman in Paris, (he was wearing a beret in the photograph) dated 1945…she surmised that he wanted to stay longer. "Surely this wasn't a woman he never got over?" she contemplated.

CHAPTER 27

THE GOLF CLUB CAPER

Louie came striding into the Driftwood, downtown East Jordan, waterfront dining. Louie was 24 years old today, July 28, 1963. It was Friday night, everything all right. Louie wore a brand new white T-Shirt, tight black jeans, creased and rolled up at the cuff, black leather Dingo boots and black wrap around shades. His dark hair was slicked back and his comb stuck out from a back pocket. He was showered, shaved and ready.

He took a stool at the end of the bar. A great location to survey the scene. Almost 9 o'clock. The last of the All-U-Can-Eat Fish Fry crowd had rolled out the door.

The house band had begun hauling in the amps and instruments and a bouncer positioned himself at the door, checking I. D.

The bartender walked down and asked, "What'll it be?"

"Usual," Louie answered.

The bartender had seen Louie around town but he was by no means a regular and the bartender has no idea what the "usual" might be.

"O. K. I'll play along," he thought. He pulled a schooner of Pabst Blue Ribbon draft with an inch head and put it in front of his customer. Louie nodded.

Louie watched as the bouncer checked the I. D.s of three college kids and questioned them about dates of birth and addresses. The three passed the test and snuck over to a table in the back. They were all dressed in the preppy uniform of the day-white Levis; Madras guaranteed to bleed short sleeve shirts and frat boots. Long blonde hair swooshed down over their foreheads to their eyebrows.

"Man, I thought he was going to catch us," one said.

"Naw. I told you these I.D.s are great.

You memorize your name, address and date of birth and they gotta let you in," his friend answered.

"Well, they sure caught us up in Charlevoix, didn't they?" the third said, shaking his head.

"That had nothing to do with I.D.s," the second kid answered. "That was that asshole what's his name's dad busting us to the bartender."

"Well, anyhow. I got three bucks," minor number one observed.

"Let's get a pitcher," number three suggested.

The three were up North for the summer, God's Country, working long hours for minimum wage at a private Charlevoix golf club, courtesy of Daddy pulling some strings.

"Son, the important and influential connections you make there will be far greater compensation than any bi-weekly wage you may earn," each had been told.

The boys soon learned that this "far greater compensation" didn't keep them in gas and beer, even with Daddy's allowance and a rent-free cabin.

"Man, we gotta get some money," the ring leader said.

"Tell me about it. I took Susan over to the Algonquin to impress her," number two lamented.

"You mean to get you some," number two retorted.

The first kid blushed, then joined the others in some boisterous laughter.

"Anyhow, I took Susan to the Algonquin. Good food, reasonable price. She orders the Captain's platter, can you believe it? Two dozen shrimp, boiled and fried. Do you know how much that is? I ordered a house salad and a bowl of chicken noodle soup. She eats 5 shrimp, if that, doesn't offer me any, gets a doggy bag and is ready to go. I dropped her off at her cottage before the sun had even set," he moaned.

"Like I said we gotta find some money."

"Check out the greaser at the bar. What a dinosaur," number three said, nodding toward the far end of the bar.

"Watch this. I think we just found our meal ticket."

The ringleader walked over to the bar, and carried on a brief conversation with Louie and then escorted him back to their table. Introductions all round and Louie was poured a fresh glass of beer. Some idle conversation and some more beer. Then the ringleader cut to the chase.

"So Louie. I can tell you know what's going on around here. I mean where can we go and have some fun. Booze. Broads. Where's the action?"

Louie was not about to let this opportunity with the loser college kids go by and feeling sentimental, longing for the "good old days," he made a strong effort to impress them, hang out, become friends, and meet some coeds.

"I'll tell you what," Louie said.

"We'll go on a little scavenger hunt. See what we can find. How's that sound?"

"Let's roll." The three stood up and drained their glasses.

"Meet you out front," Louie said. As he walked toward his ride, Louie had second thoughts but he pushed them to the back of his mind. He could do this. Louie pulled onto the main drag in his beat up, white ice cream truck, where he stored his beer. He drove slowly past the Driftwood entrance. Soon he saw headlights speeding up behind him in the rearview mirror. The three guys pulled up next to him in a bright red, 1960 Mustang convertible.

"Let's party!"

"Whew, whew, whew, lead the way," they shouted.

Louie drove out of town on M-66 along the south arm of Lake Charlevoix. After five or six miles he turned left onto a gravel road, up into the bluffs overlooking the lake.

The Mustang followed, swerving back and forth, slowing down, and speeding up. After a few turns they passed the black topped entrance of The Quiet Loon Golf and Gun Club. A huge brown boulder with a guy swinging a golf club chiseled in it was prominent as you entered.

Louie blinked his lights, then turned them off and coasted another quarter mile along the edge of the golf course. He took a left onto a dirt two-track service drive and soon swung off between two trees and parked. The Mustang parked alongside and the three college student's hopped out.

"Follow me," he said.

The three fell in behind as Louie crossed several fairways and led them up a hill to the "Snack Shack" at the 9th green. The "Shack" offered its hoi polloi patrons not only snack foods and pop but also gourmet sandwiches and top shelf liquors.

The Old Fashioned Bloody Mary was a popular eye opener.

Louie was disappointed to find that the "Snack" was padlocked and the window securely locked. His plans thwarted.

"Step aside," the ringleader ordered.

"Let an expert work his magic."

Louie guessed that the guy had some experience picking locks. The padlock couldn't be that sophisticated. Instead, he watched in disbelief as the kid rolled up his sleeves, shook his arms loose, cracked his knuckles, took a large rock and crashed it down onto the obstreperous padlock.

The padlock held; the pine door did not. A board splintered to shreds, the door was kicked in and all three delinquents rushed in to discover what treasures they might pillage within.

Louie almost called a halt to this little escapade right then and there but he couldn't find the courage to object.

"The damage has been done. No turning back now," he reasoned.

"Wow!" one kid exclaimed.

"Look at all this booze. Johnnie Walker Red, Seagram's 7, Tanqueray, Stoli, anything you want."

They went for the Johnnie Walker first, straight shots with a Stroh's chaser. Then they found the cooler with chicken sandwiches and helped themselves to several apiece. The three ripped open bag after bag of chips, Fritos and popcorn. But the main attraction was the whiskey and the first bottle soon emptied. As the whiskey started to have its deleterious effect, they sagely switched to Vodka and continued the impromptu drunken revelry.

Louie looked on helplessly.

"Hey. Let's go find some chicks," he suggested.

The three greeted his suggestion with uncontrolled laughter.

"Chicks. Chicks. Hell, at this point I can't find my nose let alone find some chicks," one responded. Louie heard more uncontrolled laughter.

"We got to get out of here," Louie exclaimed.

"He's right," frat boy number one answered.

As if on cue, all three tried to stand, grappling for whatever hold they could purchase, without success. Time for the backup plan. The collegiate near the door managed to get up onto his hands and knees and crawl out of the Snack Shack onto the 10th tee, where he immediately tipped over and snuggled into the cool, moist grass.

The other two followed like cub bears, sound asleep in moments.

"Oh shit! What to do? What to do?" Louie pondered. His efforts to wake them were to no avail. He briefly considered driving his vehicle across the fairways, dumping them in and making his getaway. But driving across pristine golf course grass was strictly forbidden on his moral compass and, besides, he couldn't move them let alone haul them into a vehicle.

Louie's dilemma resolved itself about 3:30 A.M. The lights in the golf course clubhouse blazed on and, shortly thereafter, a golf cart whizzed by followed by the whirl of sprinklers. The greens keeper had started his shift. Louie again tried to awaken his drunken compadres without success. A light spray of water sprinkled on the drunken students. One curled into the fetal position, the second turned onto his back and luxuriated in a full frontal dousing while the third had slunk off behind the Snack Shack to points unknown.

Louie surveyed the scene of the crime. The Snack Shack looked as if a demented grizzly had burglarized it. The floor lay carpeted in empty bottles, half eaten sandwiches and snacks. The door hung crookedly on its bottom hinge. The place was totaled.

Louie went into survival mode. After a futile effort to hang the door back up, he abandoned ship.

"I gotta get outta here," he declared.

He ran back across several fairways, waded across a waist deep irrigation ditch of indeterminate muck and jogged down the two track to his ride. He peeled off his muck covered jeans and T-shirt, fished out his truck keys ("Thank God I didn't lose my truck keys."), climbed behind the wheel and started up the truck. It turned over loudly, coughed and finally came to life. He edged slowly down the two-track, lights off and, when he reached the gravel road, he sped off, in the opposite direction from the golf course entrance.

For the three college students, a night of debauchery turned into a morning of shivering and confusion as they started to wake up with the sunrise. The grounds keeper shortly discovered the vandalism and theft at the Snack Shack. He promptly conducted a quick survey of the surrounding fairways with a high-powered spotlight and roused three shadows stumbling off into the rough.

He called in a walky-talky communique' to the East Jordan Sheriff Deputy on duty. Backup alerted. The Charlevoix Sheriff picked up the call on his police radio and responded.

The Sheriff observed three young men standing in the middle of the two-track, pulled up in his 1963, black and white Ford Galaxie, hit his flasher and gave just a blurp of his siren for good measure.

Within 10 minutes the Quiet Loon Golf Club course's 9th, 10th and 11th holes were covered in a dragnet.

The Sheriff thought to himself, "What the hell pile of cow manure did I just step into?!"

In the middle of the interrogation, Louie approached through the fog. He got two car lengths past them and then took off like a bat out of hell.

One of the college guys said, "Well, there goes our ride!"

The three guys, accustomed to many a fraternity raid, raised their arms in the air and assumed the position. All three had the same thought, "This will probably be splashed across the local newspaper tomorrow!"

By dawn, the fugitives had been arrested, the damage inventoried and a thorough investigation commenced. By 10:30 A.M. the Charlevoix County Sheriff stood on the 90th District Court steps, back in Charlevoix, making a statement to passersby, tourists and a few kids roller-skating. A young Assistant District Attorney stood at his side.

CHAPTER 28

SQUIRREL WHISPERER

It was 10:00 A.M., late July, in the summer of 1963, when Roberta gazed out of the office window, did a double take, and said to Maggie, "I think your squirrel whisperer is here."

Maggie looked out the window and saw a middle-aged man, 6'2" with the beginning of a pouch, heading towards the office door. He wore a faded brown jumpsuit with attached hood, feet and a bushy tail. He was a giant awkward squirrel.

It was at that moment that Maggie remembered him. In the winter, he lived in Tallahassee in a rather run down mobile home. He was retired now. He had been a farmer a long time ago and had owned a farm between Charlevoix and East Jordan. He lost his wife and only son during the war. They died when the Japanese bombed Pearl Harbor and for a very long time he felt he existed without any real purpose in life. Then back in the late 1950s, he came to stay at the Inn during the summer, and loved to talk about nature to the children who were vacationing here. At first, the children made fun of him because he just talked about the weather and it was boring to them. In the summer of 1961, a precocious boy named Timmy started asking him more and more questions about nature. Then he really opened up to the boy and they both discovered he had a wealth of information to share about the wild-life in northern Michigan. One day, Timmy came in contact with poison ivy and was quarantined to his room, but he talked to him from his window. Timmy was amazed by all of the things he knew about squirrels. Timmy's whimpers turned into smiles.

He entered the office and introduced himself.

"Hi, I'm Ralph the Squirrel whisperer!"

He took a notepad from his briefcase and declared, "I'm here for the squirrel consultation."

He started asking Maggie some pointed questions-"Is there a void in your life that you hope to fill?"

"Don't you want to hear about my squirrel problem?" said Maggie gloomily.

"No Mam, I've learned that the squirrels are never the problem. It's the humans that are always the problem!"

"Let me tell you about the situation," said Maggie.

He replied, "Mam, I got this."

Ralph paused.

Suddenly he rose to his feet, went out the door and sat on an old tree stump where he started making chirping sounds.

Maggie watched him in disbelief. First, there was a mounting tension as he went through his mysterious squirrel whispering techniques.

She overheard him say, "It's just you and me, come out of the tree's where you have been hiding—that's right and I hear your little footsteps descending gracefully now."

One squirrel after another approached him, stopped at a safe distance, stood up on their hind haunches and stared at him in disbelief. After several minutes, the intervention seemed interminable. Maggie gave Ralph a pitying look. "It is a strange situation, is it not, to be waiting here for squirrel testimonials?" Maggie thought to herself.

The squirrels went about their business satisfied that their new brethren, Ralph, although giant in stature, posed no threat and was accepted into the squirrel community. Ralph basked in silent contentment.

The session had lasted almost an hour.

Ralph then returned to the office and reported, "Your squirrel issue is solved!"

"You can take that worrisome look off of your face Maggie. It was a silly misunderstanding. Now that they appreciate that there are behavioral boundaries that they need to respect, you will have no further problems," he says.

"How much is this gonna cost me?" Maggie asked skeptically.

"My first visit is complimentary-I don't do it for the money, I do it for the squirrels!" he exclaimed.

Maggie was dumbfounded as she watched him walk to his brown, 1960 Ford 150 pickup truck. She noticed an almost imperceptible friskiness in his step and a twitch in his ears.

As he pulled out of his parking space, the squirrel tale poked out of the driver side window and fluttered in the breeze as if waving good-bye!

Maggie asked herself, "Was that a squirrel or a man?"

CARPET & MATTRESS CLEANING DEMONSTRATION

A little later that day, Maggie had a thought of taking a nap over in a sunny corner of the office, when she heard an insistent knocking at the door. She wanted to ignore it but it just wouldn't stop. She opened the door and found a saleslady, wearing a raggedy looking black wig, black high heels, a black dress and lots of dark beige make-up. She wore a lot of fake gold costume jewelry. Maggie ushered her into the office.

She stated, "Good afternoon, my name is Miss Chambers and I represent the Curious Vacuum Company. I am here to enlighten you on the wonders of this vacuum cleaner. It can clean interiors and exteriors of homes. It has the power to clean mattresses of filthy dust mites. It has an extension hose and attachments for deep cleaning of furniture. Like the Statue of Liberty, our motto is, 'Give us your dust mites, your tired and dirty rugs, and your dust bunnies.'"

"May I demonstrate?" said Miss Chambers.

Maggie had no patience for another sales demonstration, but needing a break, thought, "What the hell. The place desperately needs vacuuming and this could be amusing."

"Sure go ahead," Maggie said.

Miss Chambers went from room to room, vacuuming floors and mattresses. She pinned her hopes on the demonstration of the power of her vacuum cleaner and the great deal she was going to give Maggie for purchasing it. Maggie had no intention of buying one but lead the lady to believe she might. After three hours of demonstrating the magnificent beast, all prepared to close the deal, the lady was escorted to the door and basically given the boot. The sales lady tried to engage Maggie in a question-and-answer session about the merits of the vacuum cleaner, but Maggie had better things to do. She thanked her profusely and shut the door. A few minutes later Maggie peeked out the office window, and the saleslady was standing by her 1959, pink Cadillac puffing away on a cigarette, probably trying to figure out her next move.

"Now, if I could only teach the squirrels how to push a vacuum," Maggie mused.

SUMMER CONCERTS

Childhood friends, Sally, Roberta and Harry spent many summer afternoons listening to the East Jordan Community Band as they played by the waterfront. Before the concert began on that warm, August day, everyone rose and with hand on heart, sang "America the Beautiful." The crowd sat in lawn chairs and listened to the band play, "God Bless America," "The Star Spangled Banner," and John Philip Sousa's, "The Stars and Stripes Forever." Stillness fell upon the waterfront late in the day, and for a moment it was easy to believe the whole world was as beautiful as the world they lived in.

Being young, they talked about everything imaginable and with great certainty. It was only when a sudden cold front moved in and the wind shifted, that they knew fall wasn't far behind. It enveloped them completely and sent them hurtling towards the nearest shelter.

CHAPTER 30

SPRINGFIELD

It was nine o'clock on the 16th day of August, 1963. Maggie sat in her office in a pensive mood, staring out the window. The early morning fog had burned off and the sun rose above the white pines. Maggie made a decision. She pushed her chair away from the desk, locked the office door, returned to her apartment and packed two green Samsonite suitcases. She threw them in the truck of the car and pulled out on M-66. The car headed downstate, destination unknown.

She pulled off at a West Branch truck stop, ordered a cup of coffee and a club sandwich. Then it came to her. She dug up all the change from the bottom of her purse, walked over to the row of black telephone booths, and made the call.

"Hello, Mabel? This is your cousin Maggie. Guess what? I'm coming to visit! Yes, to Hannibal. I'm driving. How long does it take to get there? Okay, see ya soon."

The gas station attendant at the Texaco filled up her tank and cleaned her windows. He checked her fluid levels and tire pressure, while she ran inside and bought a coke and Hostess cupcakes.

"You're all set Mam," the attendant said.

Maggie hopped in the car, rolled down the windows and cranked up the radio. She turned the dial and found Nat King Cole singing, "That Sunday, That Summer."

"Yes," Maggie sighed. "It seems to me I remember this song." She took a moment to catch her breath and became strangely silent. She was reminded of Burt, and all the times he gently kissed her neck or hand as he stood by her side. Her eyes glistened with tears.

Maggie made one overnight stop with her cousin Earl and his wife, Dorothy in Springfield, Illinois. Their St. Bernard, Huckleberry, greeted her at the front door. She looked him straight in the eyes and said, "Sit!" It did no good.

He loved lying near her chest and resting his head right on her lap.

Maggie thought to herself, "Huckleberry and Burt must be in cahoots!"

After finishing a hearty Midwestern breakfast, she left for Mabel's house.

THE HOEDOWN HITCHHIKERS

Meanwhile, back in East Jordan, rumors of the Hoedown Hitchhikers coming to town started circulating. The Hitchers name came from their hectic schedule, crossing the Midwest from upper New York State to Kansas and Minnesota. Two weeks later an ad ran in the Traverse City Beagle Newspaper and the weekly Boyne City Carouse News, a local gossip rag where the classified were "King."

The advertisements announced that four Hitchhikers would appear for a show on August 17th at the Hay Wagon in Boyne City. The popular Country & Western band featured the Fiddling Fool and Fresh Boudin. Colorful, breezy, summer dresses with slits were popular with women who came to hear the band. Sally, Andrea and Roberta planned to go.

The Fiddling Fool hoped to start his own band, and select competent Country & Western musicians who were local. This was their big chance.

LADIES NIGHT OUT

Roberta, Sally and Andrea decided it was time to go out and have some fun. They drove over to the Pub, a local hangout, in East Jordan for the leaders of tomorrow. The pub was built in 1900 and had the original tin ceiling tiles with oak beams. It had large, antique Victorian ivory glass chandeliers hanging from the ceiling. The walls were covered with lots of photographs of singers like: Elvis, Buddy Holly, Johnnie Cash, Fats Domino and Patsy Cline. At the end of the bar was a large painting of a 1955, red Chevy Bel Air. It was August 18th and "The Hoedown Hitchhikers," had a gig to play there that night.

Andrea wore jeans and a short-sleeved, low cut, red and white polka-dot blouse. Her blonde hair was styled high in a bouffant and she showed off her red nails and manicure from the Hair Hut earlier in the day. Roberta wore a pretty top with a sailor look in pink, black slacks, pink flats and a pink headband holding her soft, dark hair back. They were meeting up with Harry and a couple of his friends.

When Harry walked in all dressed up, Sally's heart fluttered. She couldn't keep her eyes off of him.

Sally readjusted her sleeveless white shirt and red slacks.

"Behave yourself," was all she kept thinking. After an hour, Harry declared, "My buddies aren't going to be able to make it. Just you and me, girls!" he said, grinning from ear to ear.

Roberta and Andrea went into the bathroom and privately gossiped about Sally flirting with Harry. Roberta found this very worrisome.

"You have to remember Roberta, Harry is committed to you," said Andrea.

Roberta returned to the table. Looking concerned, Harry said, "Where have you been?"

"Just talking to a friend," Roberta replied.

"Is there something you want to talk about?" Harry said.

"Not right now, perhaps later," Roberta shrugged. Harry leaned toward Roberta and put his arm around her shoulder. He whispered, "Come on Roberta, let's dance."

Smiling and laughing, she said, "Harry I don't know what I would do without you in my life."

Shortly before Harry and his friends retired for the evening, he tried his best to dissuade four guys seated nearby with plans to go out fishing on Lake Michigan the following day. "The weather forecast is for extremely rough water on the third-largest lake of the Great Lakes. You better not go!" Harry said emphatically. The men were unshakable in their beliefs that anything could happen to them and just dismissed what Harry had to say.

At 7:50 P.M. on Sunday, Harry heard Burt's footsteps on the creaky wood stairs of the old white house he grew up in. He loved that old house with its stone fireplace, worn, uneven oak floors, and white bead board in the kitchen and the sweet memories of his mother Maggie, kissing him good-bye every morning before he went off to school. Burt tried as best he could to keep a brave face, but Harry knew instinctively that he was bringing bad news. Burt told Harry that the fishing boat with the four guys in it had capsized and there were no survivors. Not knowing what to say, Harry started to cry. Burt could see Harry was hurting and gave him a big bear hug. The evening had a frosty edge to it so Burt placed some birch wood in the old black stove, and they both sat in the kitchen and watched the logs glisten a burnished golden brown, in and out of dancing shadow.

HANNIBAL, MISSOURI

After catching up with her cousin Mabel, and getting reacquainted with Mabel's family, Maggie was ready to see the sights of Hannibal. Hannibal, Missouri is the birthplace of Samuel Clemens, i.e. Mark Twain and it played a prominent role in his literature. Tourist attractions include his birthplace, Becky Thatcher's childhood home, the white picket fence and a cave featured in Tom Sawyer could be viewed.

The mighty Mississippi flows past Hannibal and throughout Twains literature.

By 7:30 P.M., Maggie began pacing the family room. Mabel's family continued to watch TV, and it was clear that the evening was winding down. Maggie needed to get out. She did not travel over 600 miles to watch cousin Mabel view the "Red Skelton Show."

"I'm running out to get some snacks," Maggie announced. "That IGA stays open 'til nine o'clock doesn't it?"

"Yes, nine o'clock. But you better hurry. If it's slow they have been known to close up early."

Maggie hurried out the door.

"Ah, freedom," she thought. She took a momentary glimpse at the clear night sky, hopped in her car and headed into town.

She pulled into the IGA and picked up chips, dip, Frito's and seven up. At the checkout, she grabbed some Baby Ruths and Almond Joys for her private stash.

"Looks like a party. You from around these parts?" The cashier asked.

"I'm visiting my cousin Mabel out on Stevensville Road. Thought I would swing into town, pick up some snacks and see what's going on."

"How nice," he observed with an amused expression.

Maggie deposited her treats in the car, glanced at her make-up and hair in her rearview mirror, locked the car up and proceeded to stroll downtown.

"I'll find some cute little shops to investigate tomorrow," Maggie thought. The first block consisted of a pawnshop, an auto parts store, a TV repair shop and several vacant storefronts.

A party store sat on the corner of the next block. A group of juveniles loitered outside, smoking and horsing around. They barely moved to let Maggie pass.

Then came a dime store with faded out displays and advertisements in its storefront window.

Next was the Suds Saloon. Its open door beckoned to a certain select clientele. Raucous laughter, twanging country music and billowing cigarette smoke welcomed perspective patrons.

A Salvation Army store and misplaced yarn shop completed the block. Maggie continued, somewhat discouraged. A three story, red brick hotel sat on the corner of the next block.

"How convenient," Maggie thought glibly. A lady no longer of tender years decorated the doorway. Maggie saw things she had never seen before. That night, as Maggie stared into the windows, she felt unsettled when she saw clandestine figures running from shadow to shadow, slipping through the portals of the hotel of ill repute.

Maggie hurried past. Two more bars and a boarded up storefront came next. Before Maggie could cross the street, a 1963, white, Lincoln convertible slowed alongside of her and a sleazy looking guy called out, "Hi ya miss, can you help me find what I'm lookin for?"

Maggie broke out into a slow trot, crossed at the light and head-ed back to her car as fast as her legs would carry her. Breathless, she reached her car. She gave a big sigh of relief as she slid into the driver's seat and locked her doors.

"Oh dear. Hannibal is not at all as I imagined."

Early the next morning, Maggie pulled her pink pedal pushers on and a white sleeveless shirt. She grabbed her pale blue pocket book and checked her wallet to make sure she had cash. She head-ed home to northern Michigan.

As she passed the West Branch exit, she turned on the radio dial and heard Ella Fitzgerald singing, "Time After Time." In that serene moment she realized how much she loved Burt. For the first time in her life, Maggie understood the unfailing love Burt had for her.

CHAPTER 31

WHAT DOES LIFE REALLY MEAN

The chest pressure grew rapidly into a crushing pain, Burt's left arm went numb and he began to feel shortness of breath.

He searched for nitroglycerin in his tan Car hart bib overalls, "Dammit."

"How many pockets did these bib overalls have?" Scrambling frantically, Burt finally found the small round container of nitro. His hands trembling, Burt got the pillbox open and put the pill under his tongue.

An almost instant relief surged through his chest. "Why in hell am I doing this work?" Burt thought.

Burt had been assigned the task of fixing a leaking water line. With a quick inspection, he determined that the leak came from the crawl space underneath the Inn.

"Great, just great," Burt thought.

The job required a maintenance man crawling on his belly, hauling toolbox, pipe wrenches and new PVC pipes of several different lengths. Once under the Inn, you did not want to crawl out again for more tools or supplies--with the spring run off the soil had turned to muck. It stunk.

"How many times had Burt told Maggie that a heavy duty plastic vapor cover would eliminate much of the musty smell that had pervaded the Inn in the spring?" Burt thought to himself.

But it never happened. The crawl space was a veritable history in the 20th century. Plumbing pipes of copper, iron and PVC snaked under the floorboards.

Bugs, spider webs and probably the occasional snake compounded the task of deciphering this labyrinth of plumbing.

A hornet nest was built in a corner by an air vent. He crawled on his belly one foot at a time.

Burt managed to scooch out of the crawl space and sat down on a nearby Adirondack chair.

"Relief."

Soon enough Maggie walked by, snippers in hand, trying to look busy.

"I know somebody that looks like you, who works here once in a while," she commented.

"On break. Part of the benefits package," Burt chided back.

"What benefits package? I never got any benefits package," Maggie replied.

"Union," Burt answered.

Burt rose up out of the chair, made a sharp left turn and headed toward the management office.

After a brief rest, Burt headed to the workshop to find a large saw.

I CAN BE YOUR HENRY ADERMAN

The ER doctor inquired, "What exactly was he doing prior to coming here?"

"He was cutting down a tree and had chest pain," Maggie said.

"I told him in no uncertain terms not to over exert himself!" the doctor asserted.

The doctor mumbled, "Cutting up an oak tree without a chain saw! Just what the doctor ordered."

Maggie was emotionally distraught. She took advantage of his generosity to get as much work out of him as she could. She took no interest in his medical history or, for that matter, in his life during the past several decades.

"What have I done to this man?" she wondered.

Maggie waited nervously in the ER waiting room and took time to look back at their relationship over the years. Yes, he had been a thorn in her side growing up, but throughout adulthood, he had been in and out of her life and stood by her through a lot of chaos and troubles. She had taken advantage of his strong work ethic and big heart.

She could always count on Burt to come through for her. Now she realized that she had taken his friendship for granted. She couldn't deny how guilty she felt.

Later that night, sitting in the hospital room next to Burt, as he lay sleeping, Maggie decided to let go of all of the traces of disillusionment, fear and sorrow that robbed her of joy and the love she felt for Burt for so long. The next day, Maggie was resolved to tell Burt about all her regrets and feelings for him.

Maggie knew in her heart that she could never endure the loss of Burt.

EPILOGUE

A few weeks later, Burt was much improved. He came home and the following Sunday he attended church with Maggie. As they walked down the aisle, they passed by Harry and Roberta, Chef Claude, Sally, Andrea, Louie and Bob. Their faces seemed to light up a bit. Burt led Maggie to a pew and they sat down. Pastor Dandoy introduced the choir. They sang the hymn, "Here I Am Lord." Burt took Maggie's hand in his in a silent moment of tenderness.

NOTES

[1] Milton Whitmore, (Woods-N-Water News, 2012), 2.

[2] George Secord, *East Jordan Remembers* (Boyne City, Michigan: Harbor House Publishers, Inc., 1996), 1.

[3] Ibid., 1.

[4] *Historic Charlevoix* (Boyne City, Michigan: Harbor House Publishers, Inc., 1991), 42.

[5] Milton Whitmore, (Woods-N-Water News, 2012), 1.

[6] Virginia Kaake-Giacomelli, *East Jordan Remembers* (Boyne City, Michigan: Harbor House Publishers, Inc., 1996), 62.

[7] William H. Ohle, *How It Was in Horton Bay* (Charlevoix County, Michigan: 1989), 63.

[8] Jeffrey L. Rodengen, *The Legend of Chris-Craft* (Write Stuff Syndicate, Inc/Write Stuff enterprises, LLC, 1993), 116.

[9] Ibid., 116.

[10] Simon Baatz, Smithsonian, *Criminal Minds, adapted from For the Thrill of It: Leopold, Loeb, And the Murder That Shocked Chicago* (New York: HarperCollins, 2008), 72.

ABOUT THE AUTHOR

Cynthia Williams is a writer, artist and author. She is a recipient of the 2014 Ford Foundation, Ford Motor Company, Ford Freedom Award, for exemplifying, in her memoir and charitable efforts, how the power of perseverance helped her endure the challenges of her family and her life. The Ford Freedom Award was presented at the Music Hall for the Performing Arts in Detroit, Michigan. Other 2014 award recipients included Lt. Colonel (Retired) Alexander Jefferson of the Tuskegee Airmen, Civil Rights Activist Myrlie Evers-Williams and Former President of South Africa, Nelson Mandela. Her first book, *Growing Up in the D: My Grandfather, My Mother, and Me,* was published in 2013, and shortly after she was interviewed on WRCJ, 90.9 FM, Detroit Public Radio, by Program Director, and on air Host, Dr. David Wagner.

Cynthia is also an accomplished professional artist specializing in nautical and seascape oils.

She is the author of two works, including *Growing Up in the D: My Grandfather, My Mother, and Me* and *The Whispering Pines Inn.* Cynthia lives in Northville, Michigan.

View her website at: cynthiawilliamsweb.wordpress.com

ABOUT THE ILLUSTRATOR

Richard Cruger worked for General Motors for thirty years in prototype engineering. Richard holds a B.F.A. in Sculpture from Wayne State University. Richard has spent his lifetime in Detroit creating art. From magic and cardboard illusions in grade school, to scenery and props while studying at Wayne State University in Detroit, he has tried to find ways to interpret what rumbles through his brain. He uses whatever techniques and materials that help illustrate his ideas. In his years in car design and fabrication he learned skills that he still uses in his art—clay, woodworking, metal craft, mold making, plastics, graphics and stereo lithography. One small book he made 25 years ago prompted a change in the direction of his work. He began exploring artist books to interpret his ideas. The success of a 2003 show in Tokyo encouraged him to continue. In 2005 he began a long distance collaboration with Yasuo Tanaka, a Japanese artist. Having never met in person, they spent years communicating by postal mail. They conceived a project that would use trick photography to capture similar scenes of Tokyo and Detroit. They published the book PARALLEL UNIVERSE, and in 2011 they had a joint show BONES in Michigan. Currently he is using the figures that he and Tanaka have developed to create automatons and Bunraku puppets to be used in film.

Richard Cruger has won numerous awards: XE 5/2005/ Honorary mention/Annual Publishers Book and Media Show/ Chicago Illinois, BuzzWatt/2003/Award of Excellence/Annual Publishers Book and Media Show/Chicago Illinois, and AUTObiography/1997/Award of Excellence/Annual Publishers Book and Media Show/Chicago Illinois.

In addition to numerous exhibitions and commissions, Richard Cruger lectures at Cranbrook Auto Show Artists located at Cranbrook Art Museum. View his website at: dickcruger.com